JN126095

Jonathan Swift as a Conservative Trimmer

An Ideological Reading of His English Politico-Religious Writings, 1701-1726

Wataru Nakajima

中島　渉

Academic Publication Series
of the Institute of Humanities, Meiji University

明治大学人文科学研究所叢書

KINSEIDO

Contents

Chapter 3

Chapter 4

Acknowledgments

This volume is based on my PhD dissertation submitted to Sophia University in 2016, to which some necessary amendments and refinements have been made for publication.

When I look back on my academic career, the ten years at my alma mater as undergraduate and postgraduate student right at the turn of the twenty-first century provided me with numerous precious chances and lessons to train myself to be a scholar. My mentor, Professor Emeritus Akio Kobayashi, opened my eyes to the fascinating world of English literature and culture through his instruction and his books, for which I cannot express enough appreciation. The thoughtful guidance of my chief examiner, Professor Kazuhiko Funakawa, by whose expertise I have been overwhelmed, lent an essential impetus to the completion of the thesis. Critical comments by Professor Shitsuyo Masui and Professor Dominic Cheetham yielded illuminating insights into further development of the present study.

I am grateful to both Professor Emeritus Koji Watanabe of Kobe University and Professor Dr. Hermann J. Real, Director of the Ehrenpreis Centre for Swift Studies at Westfälische Wilhelms-Universität Münster, for sending me continued academic encouragement to work on a novel approach to exploring the world of the Dean of Saint Patrick's Cathedral, Dublin. Professor Noriyuki Harada of Keio University, now President of the English Literary Society of Japan, has given me the warmest support possible to enhance my research activities and deepen my intellectual and human exchanges, without which I could not have reached the stage I am at today.

Special thanks are also due to my colleagues and friends in the School of Commerce at Meiji University: Professor Emeritus James R. Bowers and Professor Brian G. Rubrecht devotedly helped me to improve my non-native English; Ms. Yasue Yokota brought me an inspiring encounter with the works of the Marquess of Halifax, which gave me a fresh perspective on my research; Professor Taro Ishiguro, Professor Yoriko Izumi, and Professor Yoko Kitada showed me much kindness in their own ways — academically and/or spiritually — which accelerated my efforts to publish these literary findings. Of course, never will I forget the words of exhortation by Professor Emeritus iv

Kazuyuki Shimotani in the School of Agriculture, which bolstered my morale to push through the long road to the doctorate.

I wish to convey my heartfelt gratitude to the late Dr. Yoichi Kaneko, a gifted and lamented Fieldingesque, who lured me into the study of eighteenth-century English literature, and to his parents, who kindly offered to let me make the best use of part of his book collection.

This volume contains revised and reworked versions of studies which first appeared in the following publications, and much is owed to the courtesy and advice of the editors and the reviewers:

"Charles I's *Answer to the Nineteen Propositions* and English Mixed Monarchy." *Asterisk*, vol. 22, 2013, pp. 53–63.

"How to Represent the Character and Conduct of 'Robin the Trickster': A Comparison of Defoe's and Swift's Vindications of the Harley Ministry." *Asterisk*, vol. 23, 2014, pp. 44–57.

"The Inherent Conservatism of a Supposed Middle-of-the-Roader: Halifax's Views on the British Political Constitution in *The Character of a Trimmer*." *Bulletin of Arts and Sciences, Meiji University*, no. 438, 2008, pp. 97–110.

"Jonathan Swift's Adherence to Mixed Monarchy: Reflections on His Early Career as a 'Conservative' Political Thinker." *Bulletin of Arts and Sciences, Meiji University*, no. 460, 2011, pp. 205–20.

"Jonathan Swift's Ideal Nation in His Unpublished Political Tracts, 1713–15." *Studies in English Literature* (Japanese Number), vol. 82, 2005, pp. 109–28.

"Modern Interpretation of Jonathan Swift's Politics: A Survey." *Toho Gakuen School of Music Faculty Bulletin*, vol. 32, 2006, pp. 149–55.

"National Problems in Jonathan Swift's Tory Tracts: An Analysis of *The Examiner* and *The Conduct of the Allies*." *Sophia English Studies*, no. 30, 2005, pp. 17–31.

"The Political Ideals of Robert Harley: Moderate Conservatism in His *Plaine English*." *Bulletin of Arts and Sciences, Meiji University*, no. 445, 2009, pp. 145–56.

"*A Tale of a Tub* and Jonathan Swift's Politico-Religious Position." *Asterisk*, vol. 21, 2012, pp. 1–9.

    Thanks to the support of the 2015/16 Special Researcher System by Meiji University, I was able to finish the first draft of my thesis. It has now turned into this book, probably the first single-authered one in English on Jonathan Swift by a Japanese scholar, and has become a part of Meiji daigaku jimbun-kagaku-kenkyu-jo sosho [Academic Publication Series of the Institute of Humanities, Meiji University]. I sincerely appreciate these scholarly and financial aids, and I would like to extend my grateful acknowledgment to Mr. Keigo Kobayashi of the Research Promotion and Intellectual Property Office in the Research Promotion Division at Meiji University, who is in charge of our Institute of Humanities, and Mr. Kyuta Sato of Kinseido Publishing for their dedicated efforts to patiently guide me at every hard step of this publication.

Abbreviations

ANP	[Charles I], "Extracts from *His Majesties Answer to the XIX. Propositions of Both Houses of Parliament*," *English Constitutional Theory and the House of Lords, 1556–1832*, by Corrine Comstock Weston, Routledge, 2010, pp. 261–65.*
CE	Jonathan Swift, *The Cambridge Edition of the Works of Jonathan Swift*, general editors, Claude Rawson et al., Cambridge UP, 2008– , 6 vols. to date.
Character	[George Savile], *The Character of a Trimmer, The Works of George Savile, Marquis of Halifax*, edited by Mark N. Brown, vol. 1, Clarendon P, 1989.
Correspondence	Jonathan Swift, *The Correspondence of Jonathan Swift, D.D.*, edited by David Woolley, Peter Lang, 1999–2014, 5 vols.**
Journal	Jonathan Swift, *Journal to Stella*, edited by Harold Williams, 2 vols., *PW*, vols. 15–16.
NP	"The Nineteen Propositions, 1 June 1642," *The Stuart Constitution, 1603–1688: Documents and Commentary*, edited by J. P. Kenyon, 2nd ed., Cambridge UP, 1986, pp. 222–26.
PC	[Henry Parker?], *A Political Catechism, English Constitutional Theory and the House of Lords, 1556–1832*, by Corrine Comstock Weston, Routledge, 2010, pp. 267–79.
PW	Jonathan Swift, *The Prose Writings of Jonathan Swift*, general editor, Herbert Davis, Basil Blackwell, 1939–74, 16 vols.**
Robinson Crusoe	Daniel Defoe, *The Life and Strange Surprizing Adventures of Robinson Crusoe (1719)*, edited by W. R. Owens, Pickering and Chatto, 2008.
Secret History	Daniel Defoe, *The Secret History of the White-Staff (1714)*, *Party Politics*, edited by J. A. Downie, Pickering and Chatto, 2000, pp. 263–94.

Shortened Titles of Swift's Works

Argument	*An Argument to Prove, That the Abolishing of Christianity in England, May, as Things Now Stand, Be Attended with Some Inconveniences, and Perhaps, Not Produce Those Many Good Effects Proposed Thereby*
Conduct	*The Conduct of the Allies, and of the Late Ministry, in Beginning and Carrying on the Present War*
Discourse	*A Discourse of the Contests and Dissensions between the Nobles and the Commons in Athens and Rome, with the Consequences They Had upon Both Those States*
Enquiry	*An Enquiry into the Behaviour of the Queen's Last Ministry, with Relation to Their Quarrells among Themselves, and the Design Charged upon Them of Altering the Succession of the Crown*
Examiner	*The Examiner*
Gulliver's Travels	*Travels into Several Remote Nations of the World*
History	*The History of the Four Last Years of the Queen*
Memoirs	*Memoirs, Relating to That Change Which Happened in the Queen's Ministry in the Year 1710*
Project	*A Project for the Advancement of Religion, and the Reformation of Manners*
Sentiments	*The Sentiments of a Church-of-England Man, with Respect to Religion and Government*
Some Free Thoughts	*Some Free Thoughts upon the Present State of Affairs*
Tale	*A Tale of a Tub*

* As the need arises, the text is collated and corrected with "The King's Answer to the Nineteen Propositions, 18 June 1642," *The Stuart Constitution, 1603–1688: Documents and Commentary*, edited by J. P. Kenyon, 2nd ed., Cambridge UP, 1986, pp. 18–20.
** Unless otherwise stated, Swift's prose is cited from *PW*, with corresponding consultation of *CE* where necessary, and the letters from *Correspondence*.

Introduction

Jonathan Swift (1667–1745) is famous, or perhaps notorious, for his opportunistic stance toward party allegiance. Numerous scholars have argued about the true meaning and intention of his partisan literary activities, but his noted conversion from Whig to Tory has stirred up endless controversy over the angle from which his political writings should be interpreted — or more simply put, whether he was a Whig or a Tory, or otherwise something else that would require a new approach, sometimes at risk for being outrageous.

Swift was on the Whig side when he first came to London in 1701 with a view to improve his social status by gaining the favor of its leading figures. Against all expectations, he received the cold shoulder from them, and in 1710 he switched to supporting the Tory ministry led by Robert Harley, 1st Earl of Oxford and Earl Mortimer (1661–1724), who invited him to be one of the chief agents in his propaganda machine. To fend off criticism from both parties, Swift's political discourses are habitually contrived to look double-edged, which has made it more difficult to reach a clear-cut conclusion on his political standpoint.

Ian Higgins, in his controversial *Swift's Politics: A Study in Disaffection*, sorts out the long-standing contradictory interpretations of Swift's political character: [1] "Swift is a post-Revolution Tory who was temporarily associated by circumstance with the Whigs"; [2] Swift is "a paradoxical, idiosyncratic political figure whose political attitudes include elements from Tory and Whig extremes of contemporary argument"; [3] "Swift is essentially a Whig in state politics and remained so despite his 'conversion' to the predominantly Tory administration of 1710–14" (2). The second account, to see Swift as a neutral moderate, is rather a minority opinion as it tends to be criticized as a naive reading of his politics. In contrast, the Tory and Whig readings are constantly adopted and compared by researchers at the forefront: a typical example is the juxtaposition of F. P. Lock and J. A. Downie.

Lock asserts that Swift was "a natural tory whose background and connections kept him in the whig fold until he realised his true political home" (*Swift's Tory Politics* 134). As to Swift's political ambiguity, he expounds:

> Swift had the misfortune to be a "natural" Tory who held certain moderate "Whig" intellectual convictions. [. . .] By temperament Swift was a Tory, inclined to pessimism, to a distrust of innovation, and to a nostalgic attachment to the values (including the political values) of the past. Temperament would finally triumph over intellectual conviction. ("Swift and English Politics" 127)

For Lock, Swift upheld "conservative and authoritarian" political values at heart (*Swift's Tory Politics* 179), typified by "order, stability and hierarchy" (136), and he "remained remarkably constant throughout his long involvement in politics" (169). This Tory interpretation literally accepts his party conversion, and in a sense it can be regarded as a conventional appreciation of his political statements.

On the other hand, Downie sees Swift as "a whig who also supported the established Church" (*Robert Harley* 127), and "professed a belief in contract theory, not in an 'ancient constitution'" (128). His analysis prefers to emphasize a rather liberal image of Swift, who "believed in the protection of liberty and property, and championed the rights and privileges of the individual against the oppression of either a king or a ministry" (*Jonathan Swift* 259–60). Swift aspired to get the patronage of the Crown in the late Stuart period, but he "stood out against arbitrary monarchy and the abuse of prerogative" (260). Like Lock, Downie insists that Swift "was not inconsistent. He did not markedly alter his political opinions on entering Harley's camp" (*Robert Harley* 128).

Judging the Whig interpretation as "a modern scholarly orthodoxy" (*Swift's Politics* 2), Higgins detaches himself from these established theories. The crucial but puzzling point is that the "[t]wo authoritative scholars [. . .] have arrived at spectacularly opposed verdicts on Swift's politics," in spite of "[rehearsing] much the same evidence in their historical criticism of Swift's texts" (4). Higgins raises an objection to the "conceptions of Swift as a Whig" and "a non-Jacobite Tory" alike (ix), and offers the innovative view that Swift has a Jacobite inclination, in consonance with the contemporary High-Church Tory cause (7–8, 37). Although Higgins concedes that "[w]hether or not Swift was a Jacobite cannot be determined" (ix), he points to the "[e]choes of the proscribed Jacobite voice in the political polyphony of Swift's culture" (x). This is quite an ambitious and radical exposition of Swift's politics, and it still provokes ceaseless argument.

So far, each type of interpretation has long carried a respective power of persuasion, but all the more because of that, the topic of Swift's political stance has been almost destined to be inconclusive.[1] Hence the central purpose of this study is to propose that we should more closely examine and abstract the consistent and commonly observed features in Swift's partisan writings before and after his conversion, and that, by adopting a viewpoint of the history of political thought, we will be able to embrace and place his politics in another comprehensible category, namely, conservatism, above his two-faced partisanship.

In this connection, it is worthy of attention that Anthony Quinton lays out a history of conservative thought in England in *The Politics of Imperfection: The Religious and Secular Traditions of Conservative Thought in England from Hooker to Oakeshott*. With respect to the early modern period, he stretches the lineage from Richard Hooker (1554?–1600) — via Thomas Hobbes (1588–1679) as "a digression"; Edward Hyde, 1st Earl of Clarendon (1609–74); George Savile,

1st Marquess of Halifax (1633–95); Henry St John, 1st Viscount Bolingbroke (1678–1751); David Hume (1711–76); and Samuel Johnson (1709–84) — to Edmund Burke (1729–97). The lineup is suitable at first glance and chosen without relation to their occupation: it includes theologian, philosopher, politician, and even litterateur. Indeed Quinton's attempt, though brief, makes a valuable contribution toward forming and offering a sketch of conservative history in the face of the prevalence of "progressive" Whig interpretation of history. It seems quite odd, however, that the two conspicuous apparent opportunists in the early years of the eighteenth century — Harley and Swift — are excluded from the list, in spite of possessing the same characteristics as Halifax, the most prominent "Trimmer," who has generally been treated as a minor figure in this area. As the primary principle of conservatism, Quinton picks up traditionalism, which is represented in the deference to "established customs and institutions," and the "hostility to sudden, precipitate and, *a fortiori*, revolutionary change" (16).[2] By his definition conservatism itself is essentially different from reactionism, immobilism, totalitarianism, and absolutism (19–21), and its core lies in the preference for "law and 'mixed government,'"[3] so as not to give "absolute power" either to "the individual" or "the state" (22). Now what is important is that, on the basis of this assumption, Swift should be properly qualified to be recognized as a conservative thinker.[4] As we shall discuss later, Swift, whose political pamphlets show a potent influence of Harley, persistently espouses mixed monarchy to protect the national polity of Britain regardless of party affiliation, like Halifax.

In this study, therefore, I would also like to clarify the precise nature of Swift's advocacy of this ancient constitution and reveal that he deserves to carry on the tradition of conservative political thought beyond the simple Tory-Whig dichotomy. I shall concentrate on his English writings, especially around the end of the Stuart dynasty, for his fundamental political ideals were established during these golden days as an active ministerial pamphleteer, and they later contributed to constituting an essential part of his literary masterpiece, *Gulliver's Travels* (1726).

In chapter 1, we will investigate the extent to which Swift upheld the concept of mixed monarchy, with an intensive focus on *A Discourse of the Contests and Dissensions between the Nobles and the Commons in Athens and Rome, with the Consequences They Had upon Both Those States* (1701), known as his memorable first political tract. The *Discourse* lays out his basic idea of the system of government. He wrote it as a Whig writer, but it gives us a whole picture of his ideal of the state beyond party lines. We will find that his championship of the mixed constitution shares a common ground with the nonpartisan appeal by Halifax for defending the English national polity, which was designed in *The Character of a Trimmer* (writ. 1684, pub. 1688). On top of that, we will look into how the theory of the ancient constitution developed and functioned in the political circles between the two revolutions in the seventeenth-century, to show that it has its classical roots traced back to Polybius (c. 200–c. 118 BC), and that it was utilized for supporting the conservative cause of constitutional governance. *His Majesties Answer to the Nineteen Propositions of Both Houses of Parliament* (1642), issued in the reign of Charles I (1600–49; r. 1625–49), was the key to stabilizing the contemporary ideological conflict between monarchism and parliamentarism, and Halifax and Swift cannot be spared from its impact.

Chapter 2 deals with Swift's views on the relation between religion and politics. As a first step, we will reexamine the text and the context of *A Tale of a Tub* (1704). There is still enough room to challenge Higgins's provocative reading, which emphasizes Swift's commitment to Jacobitism, because we cannot overlook the fact that Swift was a clergyman of the Church of Ireland yet had an ardent ambition to hold an important post in the Church of England. It can hardly be expected that he stood loyally for James II (1633–1701; r. 1685–88), who was notorious for his Catholic faith. Even if Swift, suspected of xenophobia, may have been dissatisfied with a foreign (though Protestant) king, William III (1650–1702; r. 1689–1702), who was tolerant of Dissenters, it seems unlikely that his adherence to Anglican polity would allow him to accept the prevalence of Catholicism. The *Tale* is estimated to have been written between 1696 and 1698 (Hashinuma 61), when both James and William were still alive. Given this perspective, Swift's deep antipathy toward Jacobite rule will be demonstrated, thereby countering Higgins's insistence on his advocacy of Jacobitism. The Anglican establishment is a central pillar of Swift's ideal political structure, and we will see him affirm the Revolution settlement that had ousted James. In order to substantiate Swift's persistent claim to Anglicanism, we will then turn our attention to his religious tracts written around the time of Harley's temporary fall from power, which would fatefully affect the partisanship of both men, in 1708. Laid on the table will be *The Sentiments of a Church-of-England Man, with Respect to Religion and Government* (writ. 1708, pub. 1711); *An Argument to Prove, That the Abolishing of Christianity in England, May, as Things Now Stand, Be Attended with Some Inconveniences, and Perhaps, Not Produce Those Many Good Effects Proposed Thereby* (writ. 1708, pub. 1711); and *A Project for the Advancement of Religion, and the Reformation of Manners* (1709). Later in *Memoirs, Relating to That Change Which Happened in the Queen's Ministry in the Year 1710* (writ. 1714, pub. 1765), Swift particularly named them as his anti-Low-Church efforts in retrospect of his early career (*PW* 8: 122), and they illustrate his moderate stance toward polarized partisan and sectarian fray. Also noteworthy is that Swift treated Hobbes as his ideological enemy: we will make a comparative review of their visions of church and state and disclose Swift's competitive antipathy toward anticlericalism and the denial of the mixed government expounded in *Leviathan* (1651).

In chapter 3, we will obtain an overview of the transformation of party ideologies after the Glorious Revolution (1688–89) and observe an overall trend of conservatization which blurred the border between Toryism and Whiggism in the political world. On that basis, we will focus on Swift's two important Tory-commissioned tracts: *The Examiner* (1710–11; nos. 13–45) and *The Conduct of the Allies* (1711), produced when he was active as a chief propagandist under Harley's direction. Swift's distaste for party politics and his thought on the national problems of Britain are brought into relief to give an account of the political concepts which he wanted to entrust to the Tory ministry then seizing the power of the state, rather than to determine how loyal he and his theses were to the Tories. Due consideration shall be paid to *Plaine English to All Who Are Honest, or Would Be So If They Knew How* (writ. 1708), which perceptively demonstrates Harley's political ideals (Matsuzono 186), to reveal that they took on the marked characteristics of early modern conservatism. Thus we can measure Swift's ideological closeness or distance to Harley's moderate scheme and confirm that, despite changing sides to seek his own social success, Swift consistently strove to protect the Protestant monarchical government, irrespectively of which party he supported.

Chapter 4 looks into Swift's unpublished papers written at the change of dynasty from Stuart to Hanover without commission from Harley, which explicitly and implicitly present his ideal image of national polity. As the Tory administration was thrown into crisis and finally collapsed due to its internal power struggle between his patrons Harley and St John, Swift attempted to provide historical accounts of the deeds of the Harley ministry. Unfortunately, the manuscripts could not receive material and practical support from the two leading ministers for publication and thus were not printed during his prime. Swift overvalued his relationship with the Treasurer and the Secretary of State: he believed that he had established *personal* trust with them, but his supposed friendship did not necessarily create the fullest *political* confidence. However, all the more because those works were produced without party backing, they can reflect his political views beyond party allegiance. Their potential to help us fathom his real intentions has not been fully exploited, and a closer analysis of them should further endorse the consistency of his vision of an ideal nation, as represented by the adherence to Anglicanism, the security of the Protestant succession, and the espousal of the theory of the ancient constitution. In particular, *Memoirs* will undergo a deeper examination, with a critical comparison with *The Secret History of the White-Staff* (c. 1714) by Daniel Defoe (c. 1660–1731), which is to shed fresh light on the political and literary rivalry between the two major authors and propagandists of the day. Ideological discord between *Robinson Crusoe* (1719) and *Gulliver's Travels* will also be discussed to show that Defoe's apparently liberal cast of mind could provoke Swift to continue defending conservative values against the corruption of political and religious morals, even after the loss of his social status in England in the Hanoverian period.

It is true that political action by Swift certainly looks opportunistic or trimming as well as that by Halifax, who was a declared Trimmer, and Harley, who was called Robin the Trickster, but the political thought of each "trimmer" is instrumental enough to preserve the national polity from the turmoil of civil and foreign wars. The trimmer's politics can help to keep the society from falling into radical extremes, and it is a possible form of English conservatism which would seek to take the golden mean. In this sense, Swift was capable of playing an adequate role. In the end, my approach is never to deny the established partisan readings of Swift's works, and it is hoped that it could open a new horizon for the criticism of his literary efforts.

Chapter 1

The Archetype of Swift's Political Thought

A Discourse of the Contests and Dissensions
between the Nobles and the Commons in Athens and Rome
in the Context of the Seventeenth-Century Theory
of Mixed Government

1. Swift's Ideal of the State in *A Discourse of the Contests and Dissensions in Athens and Rome*

Swift made his debut into the political world with *A Discourse of the Contests and Dissensions between the Nobles and the Commons in Athens and Rome* in 1701. His initial aim for writing it was to defend four Whigs in hot water, who were impeached for taking part in the negotiations for the Partition Treaties (1698, 1700) to settle the Spanish succession. John Somers, Baron Somers (1651–1716), a Whig leader at the time, was included there,[1] so Swift, then an obscure writer, came over to the Whig side in the hope of winning public favor as a first step to satisfy his political ambition at the center of English politics.[2] He expressed his adherence to mixed monarchy in the *Discourse* to support the Whig cause, but he was often acknowledged as an opportunist because he changed sides in pursuit of his own political interests. After Somers, Swift sought the patronage of Sidney Godolphin, 1st Earl of Godolphin (1645–1712), a leading Tory who formed the coalition government with the Junto Whigs, and then of Robert Harley, who was once Godolphin's colleague and rival, but later became the first minister of the Tory government. Despite this capricious commitment to party politics, Swift kept championing mixed monarchy, both before and after his conversion from Whig to Tory. To figure out what is behind his tricky consistency, we shall examine how he declared and developed his coherent conviction of monarchical constitution, thereby revealing his potential contribution to a conservative line of political thought through a close analysis of the *Discourse*.

The *Discourse* is composed of Swift's (rather biased) advisory account of the contemporary political situation in the form of historical reference to the politics of ancient times. Its main feature would be that he shows his firm advocacy of mixed monarchy, namely, the government that consists of Crown, Lords, and Commons. Comparing the three types of "pure" government (monarchy, aristocracy, and democracy), Swift strongly upholds the mixed constitution as the best choice:

> Now the three Forms of Government [. . .] differ only by the Civil Administration being placed in the Hands of One, or sometimes Two, (as in *Sparta*) who were called *Kings*; or in a Senate, who were called the *Nobles*; or in the People Collective or Representative, who may be called the *Commons*: [. . .] But the Power in the last Resort, was always meant by Legislators to be held in Ballance among all Three. And it will be an eternal Rule in Politicks, among every free People, that there is a Ballance of Power to be carefully held by every State within it self, as well as among several States with each other. (*Discourse, PW* 1: 196–97; ch. 1)

> [A] mixt Government [. . .] hath Place in Nature and Reason; seems very well to agree with the Sentiments of most Legislators, and to have been followed in most States, whether they have appeared under the Name of Monarchies, Aristocracies, or Democracies. [. . .] *Polybius* tells us, the best Government is that which consists of three Forms, *Regno, Optimatium, & Populi Imperio*: Which may be fairly translated, the *Kings, Lords*, and *Commons*. (199–200)

Swift's argument is premised on his deliberate definition of each of the three parties of the mixed government. In respect of Crown, he explains:

> [I]t seems to me, that a free People met together, whether by *Compact* or *Family Government*, as soon as they fall into any Acts of Civil Society, do, of themselves, divide into three Powers. The first is, that of some one eminent Spirit, who having signalized his Valour, and Fortune in Defence of his Country, or by the Practice of popular Arts at home, becomes to have great Influence on the People, to grow their Leader in warlike Expeditions, and to preside, after a sort, in their Civil Assemblies: And this is grounded upon the Principles of Nature and common Reason, which in all Difficulties and Dangers, where Prudence or Courage is required, do rather incite us to fly for Counsel or Assistance to a single Person than a Multitude. (196)

Although he consistently supports *mixed* monarchy, it is highly notable that he reveals that, in essence, monarchy by "a single Person" is the most natural system to rule the country, especially when it faces national crises. When it comes to Lords, Swift expresses as follows:

> The Second natural Division of Power, is of such Men who have acquired large Possessions, and consequently Dependances, or descend from Ancestors, who have left them great Inheritances, together with an Hereditary Authority: These easily uniting in Thoughts and Opinions, and acting in Concert, begin to enter upon Measures for securing their Properties; which are best upheld by preparing against Invasions from Abroad, and maintaining Peace at Home. This commences a great Council, or Senate of Nobles for the weighty Affairs of the Nation. (196)

The point is to share common values among the respectable class. He considers men of property to be more suitable as politicians than common people would be because the former are more unsusceptible to corruption due to their affluence.[3] With regard to Commons, Swift states rather briefly:

> The last Division is of the Mass, or Body of the People; whose Part of Power is great, and undisputable, whenever they can unite either collectively, or by Deputation to exert it. (196)

Such conciseness hints at his relative apathy and mistrust toward the multitude as a political force. In his heart, Swift seems to be inclined to kingship among the three powers in order to operate a stable government.

In fact, it is not always good to simply leave political power to a large number of people. Swift insists that it is erroneous to think that "Power is always safer lodged in many Hands than in one," and notes:

> For, if these many Hands be made up, only from one of the three Divisions before-mentioned; it is plain [. . .] and easy to be paralleled in other Ages and Countries, that they are as capable of enslaving the Nation, and of acting all Manner of *Tyranny* and *Oppression*, as it is possible for a single Person to be; although we should suppose their Number to be not only of four or five Hundred, but above three Thousand. (*Discourse*, *PW* 1: 200; ch. 1)

The important thing is to maintain balance between the three powers. If any one of them puffs up, it will cause tyranny, which, in Swift's mind, will emerge regardless of the number of people concerned. Likening the "Ballance of Power" to the mechanism of a pair of scales, he writes:

> [I]n a State within it self, the Ballance must be held by a third

Hand, who is to deal the remaining Power with the utmost Exactness into each Scale. Now it is not necessary, that the Power should be equally divided between these three; for the Ballance may be held by the Weakest, who by his Address and Conduct, removing from either Scale, and adding of his own, may keep the Scales duly poised. [. . .]

When the Ballance is broke, by the Negligence, Folly, or Weakness of the Hand that held it, or by mighty Weights fallen into either Scale; the Power will never continue long in equal Division between the two remaining Parties, but (until the Ballance is fixed anew) will run entirely into one. [. . .] [Tyranny] is not meant for the seizing of the uncontrouled, or absolute Power into the Hands of a single Person; (as many superficial Men have grosly mistaken) but for the breaking of the Ballance by whatever Hand, and leaving the Power wholly in one scale. For *Tyranny* and *Usurpation* in a State, are by no Means confined to any Number [. . .]. (197–98)

Swift admits that the power of the state is not necessarily "equally divided between these three," but the balance should be "duly" kept by a "third Hand" which can control the other two "Scales." According to the drift of his argument, the ideal "third Hand" would indicate the king as he has implicitly stressed the danger of vesting the power in the hands of plural numbers rather than "a single Person." He would mean that tyranny can be established even by aristocracy or democracy, and that would be why he sympathizes most with monarchy.

To Swift it does not matter very much "from which Door of the three [divisions]" tyranny will be "let in" when "the Ballance is broke" (*Discourse, PW* 1: 201; ch. 1). Further, he mentions that the tyranny imposed by a group, such as the Lords and the Commons, will finally result in individual tyranny,[4] because the will of a group will inevitably split:

14

> [A]bsolute Power [hath] been pursued by the several Parties of
> each particular State; wherein single Persons have met with most
> Success, although the Endeavours of the *Few* and the *Many* have
> been frequent enough: Yet, being neither so uniform in their
> Designs, nor so direct in their Views, they neither could manage
> nor maintain the Power they had got; but were ever deceived by
> the Popularity, and Ambition of some single Person. (202–03)

Nevertheless, in the light of his relative preference to monarchy, Swift
especially regards tyranny of the Commons as most dangerous, as if to
form the keynote of the *Discourse*. In fact, he repeatedly argues that
both Athens and Rome collapsed because of the excess of popular rule,
using exactly the same term, "*Dominatio Plebis*." As to Athens, whose
first possible constitution was presumed to be "rather a Sort of mixed
Monarchy than a popular State" (204; ch. 2), he remarks:

> [T]his very Power of the People in *Athens*, claimed so confidently
> for an *inherent Right*, and insisted on as the *undoubted Privilege of
> an* Athenian *born*, was the rankest Encroachment imaginable, and
> the grossest Degeneracy from the Form that *Solon* left them.[5] In
> short, this Government was grown into a *Dominatio Plebis*, or
> *Tyranny of the People*; who, by Degrees, had broke and overthrown
> the Ballance which that Legislator had very well fixed and provided
> for. (209)

Concerning Rome (before the Roman Empire, that is, from the time of
Romulus, the legendary founder of the country, to that of Gaius Julius
Caesar [100–44 BC], who practically exercised "the Tyranny of a single
Person"), Swift contends that "a limited and divided Power" was its
"most antient and inherent Principle" as in Greece, but that plebeians
gradually "[grew] into Power and Property," "[gained] Ground upon

the *Patricians*," and "overturned the Ballance," only to destroy this "wisest Republick" (211–12; ch. 3). Then he refers to the cause of its fall, basing his argument on a prediction by Polybius: "[I]ts Ruin would arise from the popular Tumults, which would introduce a *Dominatio Plebis*, or Tyranny of the People" (217). The problem is that, in Rome, the power of the Commons surpassed that of the Senate. In Swift's view, the common people in general are merely good at scrapping and rebuilding and do not care for the preservation of social order:

> From this Deduction of popular Encroachments in *Rome*, the Reader will easily judge how much the Ballance was fallen upon that Side. Indeed, [. . .] the very Foundation was removed, and it was a moral Impossibility, that the Republick could subsist any longer. For, the Commons having usurped the Offices of the State, and trampled on the Senate, there was no Government left, but a *Dominatio Plebis* [. . .].
>
> I think it is an universal Truth, that the People are much more dextrous at pulling down, and setting up, than at preserving what is fixed [. . .]. (219)

To put it another way, Swift suggests that, in order to prevent such mob tyranny, it should be required to, at the least, maintain the equilibrium of political power between the nobles and the commons, if not to hold down the commons by their superiors. To that extent, he puts a low value on the governance capacity of the masses.[6]

Now it is quite likely that Swift does not trust the discretion of the people, as he perceives how public opinion is prone to change:

> I think it a great Error to count upon the Genius of a Nation as a standing Argument in all Ages; since there is hardly a Spot of Ground in *Europe*, where the Inhabitants have not frequently and

entirely changed their Temper and Genius. Neither can I see any Reason, why the Genius of a Nation should be more fixed in the Point of Government, than in their Morals, their Learning, their Religion, their common Humour and Conversation, their Diet and their Complexion; which do all notoriously vary, almost in every Age; and may every one of them have great Effects upon Men's Notions of Government. (*Discourse*, *PW* 1: 229–30; ch. 5)

Such a sense of distrust has a substantial influence on his assessment of the two revolutions in the seventeenth century. Idealizing the reign of Elizabeth I (1533–1603; r. 1558–1603), for "the Power between the Nobles and the Commons" was "in more equal Ballance than it was ever before or since," Swift insists:

But then, or soon after, arose a Faction in *England*; which, under the Name of *Puritan*, began to grow popular, by molding up their new Schemes of Religion with *Republican* Principles in Government; who gaining upon the *Prerogative*, as well as the *Nobles*, under several Denominations, for the Space of about Sixty Years, did at last overthrow the Constitution; and, according to the usual Course of such Revolutions, did introduce a Tyranny, first of the People, and then of a single Person.

In a short Time after, the old Government was revived. But the Progress of Affairs, for almost Thirty Years, under the Reigns of two weak Princes, is a Subject of a very different Nature; when the Ballance was in Danger to be overturned by the Hands that held it; which was, at last, very seasonably prevented by the late Revolution. (230)

In the former part of this passage, his instinctive antipathy to democracy leaks out. He gives a negative evaluation to the so-called Puritan

Revolution (1642–49). Probably as a clergyman of the Church of Ireland, Swift praises the Elizabethan era, which established the Anglican Church system. Besides his hatred of Puritanism, however, he denounces *"Republican* Principles," and describes the civil war as the "overthrow" of the political constitution of England. He even labels the rule of Oliver Cromwell (1599–1658; Prot. 1653–58) — "a Tyranny [. . .] of a single Person" — as virtually "a popular Usurpation" (231). His criticism of the encroachment on the royal prerogative gives us a glimpse of his firm support on the side of the power of the kings. On the other hand, in the latter part, Swift suggestively (but intelligibly) defends the Glorious Revolution. He sarcastically reproaches the despotic-looking Catholic kings, Charles II (1630–85; r. 1660–85) and James II, for being "weak Princes," but the revolution itself can be seen to result in a conservative one to preserve the ancient constitution, rather than a civil one to allow the people to seize the power of the state (Matsuzono 105–12). It is worth noting that, though Swift is known to dislike the pro-Dissenter foreign king, William III, he implicitly acknowledges his accession to the throne and the Revolution settlement which maintains the regal government. Thus we can fairly say that Swift places top priority on the monarchical side among the three divisions of power in national politics. He even warns that the powers that be should make no concessions to the pressure from the people, reflecting on the examples of "the *Dissentions* in *Rome,* between the two Bodies of Patricians and Plebeians" (*Discourse, PW* 1: 226; ch. 4).[7]

It is true that Swift wrote the *Discourse* on behalf of the Whigs: he attempted to criticize the Tories in the Commons by comparing them to the body of plebeians, which destabilized the political world in ancient times. However, his argument about the system of governance was not essentially susceptible to party interests: never did he mean to vindicate the power of parliament, though the Whigs were originally sympathetic to parliamentary politics, nor to unconditionally appreciate the rule of the king, though the Tories were by nature supportive of the royal authority. His persistent aversion to a *"Dominatio Plebis"* brought him to object to civil revolution and champion the preservation of mixed monarchy. Such conservative desire formed the basis of his political consciousness, which would never change even after he converted to the Tory side. His twisted partisan stance and coherent conservative politics look quite unique, but we can find a valuable precedent for such an apparently opportunistic political figure in the near past, that is, George Savile, Marquess of Halifax.

2. Precursory Nonpartisan Conservatism of Halifax the "Trimmer"

Halifax wrote his most famous work, *The Character of a Trimmer*, at the very end of the life of Charles II. He was a member of the Privy Council and later the Lord Privy Seal under his reign, and was closely involved in the vortex of the Exclusion Crisis (1679–81), which gave origin to the party conflict between Whigs and Tories. The former opposed the succession of the king's brother, the Duke of York (later James II), and supported the Exclusion Bill because James was a Catholic; the latter advocated the royal authority and supported his title to the throne. Once submitted, the Bill passed the House of Commons easily, but in the Lords Halifax made eloquent speeches against it in rivalry with Anthony Ashley Cooper, 1st Earl of Shaftesbury (1621–83), founder of the Whig party and his uncle by marriage, who was eagerly committed to backing James Scott, Duke of Monmouth (1649–85), an illegitimate son of Charles. Halifax had been seen to back the Bill because he was a consistent anti-Catholic and at odds with the Duke of York. Contrary to such expectations, he opposed it, arguing that, if it were enacted, the heir presumptive would gain the cooperation of

Scotland and Ireland to rise in revolt. As this logic for persuasion — the prospective danger of civil war — touched the right chord in the Lords, already disgusted at the traumatic memory of the Puritan Revolution or the Great Rebellion, Halifax admirably turned the tables in parliament, and the Bill was finally rejected with more than double the votes of its supporters. Thus he invited fierce anger from the Whigs, but soon after he put forth a proposal to install Mary (wife of William of Orange, later Mary II [1662–94; r. 1689–94]) as regent, which provoked the disapproval of both parties. Unsurprisingly his scheme was turned down, and he lost favor also with the Tories. What Halifax managed was to keep balance: indeed, he maintained the hereditary succession on behalf of the Catholic successor, but he simultaneously promoted the Test Act (1673–1828) and tried to check the prince's increasing despotic influence. It is not to be denied that, under this settlement, Halifax made a significant contribution to preventing civil wars and defending the English national polity. Nevertheless, his nonpartisan manner inevitably aroused the hostility of various factions because he definitely appeared to be an opportunist.[8] The nickname "Trimmer" was "put upon him angrily by his contemporaries" (Raleigh vii), but he used it for justifying a detached political attitude. In the *Character*, he declares:

> This innocent Word *Trimmer* signifieth no more than this, that if men are together in a Boat, and one part of the Company would weigh it down on one side, another would make it lean as much to the contrary, it happneth there is a third Opinion, of those who conceave it would do as well, if the Boat went even, without endangering the Passengers. (179)

For Halifax, his moderate politics is not so much a noncommittal maneuvering for private advantage as a spontaneous endeavor to protect national interests beyond partisan ones.[9] The *Character* was initially circulated in manuscript around 1684, that is, in the heat of the struggle over the succession problem. It seems quite probable that Halifax attempted to make a direct appeal to Charles II to put forward his opinion on the fundamental governing system of the state (Kenyon, Introduction 12; Reed 64). As a consequence of Charles dying immediately after circulation, the tract failed to produce direct concrete results. However, it was repeatedly reprinted, not only after its publication in 1688, but also after Halifax's own death in 1695. It is little wonder that the *Character* left an indelible impression on the stream of political thought from the late seventeenth to the early eighteenth century.[10]

In spite of Halifax's efforts to propound a disinterested proposal, the overall tenor of his argument in the *Character* seems to be colored by a specific concept: his firm adherence to the preservation of a stable government that may disclose a latent inclination for conservative principles, which English society would apply at the critical moment on the heels of the publication of the tract, namely, the Glorious Revolution. We shall analyze the discourse of the *Character* on the political consti-tution and shed light on how his "neutral" ideology was more affected by the infiltration of conservatism than has generally been imagined, possibly contrary to the popular belief that the rise of liberal thought (say the Lockean theory) was a driving force for the "people's" revolution.

Halifax denounces both absolute monarchy and republicanism as "Barbarous Extreams," because "Monarchy is a thing which leaveth men no Liberty, and a Common-wealth such a one as alloweth them no quiet." He believes that the English constitution adopts "a wise mean" between them, which is what "selfe preservation ought to dictate to our wishes," and that it has "attained this mean in a greater measure, than any Nation now in being, and perhaps than any we read of, though never so much celebrated for the wisedome or the felicitie of their

Constitution" (*Character* 184). He virtually proposes a limited, mixed monarchy as the best suited form of government for England:

> Wee take from one [Monarchy] the too great power of doing hurtt, and yet leave enough to governe and protect us; Wee take from the other [Common-wealth] the Confusion, the parity, the animosities, and the Lycence, and yet reserve a due care of such a Libertie, as may consist with men's Allegiance. (184–85)

> Our *Trimmer* admireth our blessed constitution, in which dominion and Liberty are so happyly reconciled; it giveth to the Prince the glorious power of comanding freemen, and to the subjects the satisfaction of seing that power so Lodged, as that their Liberties are secure. [. . .] And as of all the orders of building the Composite is the best, so ours by a wise mixture and a happy choice of what is best in others, is brought into a forme, that is our felicitie who live under it, and the envye of our Neighbours who cannot imitate it. (194)

A mixed government consists of Crown, Lords, and Commons: it can be seen as a "Composite" of monarchism and republicanism, where parliament is expected to control the king's arbitrary power, though the scope of the Crown's authority and the power balance between the aristocracy and the people should vary with the individual thinker. Of course, this "blessed constitution" must be via media Anglican as "our Church is a *Trimmer* between the frenzie of Phanatick Visions, and the Lethargick Ignorance of Popish dreams" (243).

Halifax was said to be favorable to republicanism,[11] but the general tone of the *Character* carries his negative view on the feasibility of democracy due to the lack of capability of the masses:

The Rules of a Common-wealth are too hard for the Bulke of
Mankind to come up to; that forme of Government requireth such
a spiritt to carry it on, as doth not dwell in great numbers, but is
restrained to so very few, especially in this age, that let the methods
appeare never so reasonable in Paper, they must faile in Practice,
which will ever be suited more to men's Nature as it is than as it
should be. (185)

Here he seems to appreciate the effectiveness of republicanism in the
ultimate sense, but the political standard of the people is decisively
insufficient to achieve that height. He suggests that the political system
of the government should be settled in keeping with reality rather than
with the ideal. His sense of reality makes him insist on the danger of the
"Common-wealth" degenerating into mobocracy:

[T]here is a Soul in that great Body of the People, which may for a
time be drowsie and unactive, but when the *Leviathan* is rowsed, it
moveth like an angry Creature, and will neither be convinced nor
resisted. The people can never agree to shew their united power,
till they are extreamly tempted and provoked to it, so that to apply
cupping Glasses to a great Beast naturally disposed to sleep, and to
force the Tame thing, whether it will or noe, to be valiant, must be
learnt out of some other Book than *Machiavell*, who would never
have prescribed such a preposterous method.

　　It is to be remembred, That if Princes have Law and Authoritie
on their side, the People on theirs may have Nature, which is a
formidable Adversary. Duty, Justice, Religion, nay even human
Prudence too, biddeth the people suffer every thing rather than
resist; but uncorrected Nature, where ever it feeleth a smart, will
run to the nearest Remedy. Men's Passions are in this case to be
considered, as much as their Duty, Let it be never so strongly

enforced; for if their passions are provoked, they being as much a part of us as any of our Limbs, they lead men into a short way of arguing that admitteth no distinctions, and from the foundation of selfe defence, they will draw Inferences that will have miserable Effects upon the quiet of a Government. (241–42)

Halifax clearly places some distance between his side (presumably the aristocracy) and the people. The multitude are originally regarded as "a formidable Adversary" to the powers that be. They are likened to a "Beast" or "*Leviathan*," and he apparently hopes to keep them "drowsie and unactive" as much as possible for "the quiet of a Government." In a word, his ideal image of them is a sleeping giant, which reveals that he is reluctant to admit the people's right of resistance. Eventually he declares that "[o]ur *Trimmer* therefore dreadeth a General Discontent" and warns that "[i]n every shape it is fatall, and our *Trimmer* thinketh no paines or Precaution can be too great to prevent it" (242). The point is that in spite of recommending the mixed form of government, Halifax shows without hesitation his distrust of the people as part of a governing body.[12]

Halifax is inclined to weigh monarchism as rather a natural course for England: "it being hard if not impossible to be exactly even, our Government hath much the stronger Byasse towards Monarchy, which by the more generall consent and practice of mankind, seemeth to have the advantage in the dispute against a Common-wealth" (*Character* 185). In fact, his defense of the function of monarchy frequently appears in the *Character*. For instance, he writes:

Monarchy is liked by the People for the bells and the Tinsell, the outward Pomp and the guilding, and there must be milk for Babes, since the greater part of mankind are, and ever will be included in that List; and it is approved by wiser and more thinking men, as the best when compared with others, all Circumstances and objections impartially considered. Then it hath so great an advantage above all other forms, when the administration of that power falleth into a good hand, that all other Governments looke out of Countenance, when they are set in competition with it. (185)

Although monarchy is described as just an ostentation ("the outward Pomp") to men, Halifax never extols republicanism. Most men are like "Babes," who need to be brought up with milk; it might sound as if the people have to reach fuller maturity in order to possess and maintain a republican constitution. Thus monarchy is altogether appropriate for an infantile mankind, on condition that the power is administered by "a good hand." Halifax emphasizes that the wise, righteous sovereign is essential to operate a stable government:

[N]o Monarchy can be perfect and absolute without exception, but where the Prince is superiour by his vertues, as well as by his Character, and his power. [. . .] And it may be affirmed that the instances are very rare of Princes having the worst in the dispute with their people, if they were eminent either for Justice in time of Peace, or conduct in time of Warr; Such advantage the Crowne giveth to those who adorne and confirme it by their own peronall vertues. (186)

Due to the lingering effect of the tradition of "mirrors for princes," it was considered a popular persuasive concept from the Middle Ages through the eighteenth century that moral perfection is required of an ideal ruler (Takahama 262–69), and Halifax seems to follow that theory.[13] He repeats the necessity of "vertues" to the king:

Our *Trimmer* cannot conceave that the power of any Prince can be lasting, but where it is built upon the foundation of his own unborrowed vertue; he must not only be the first moover and the fountaine from whence all the great acts of state originally flow, but he must be thought so by his people, that may preserve their veneration to him [. . .]. (*Character* 192)

In this way, Halifax appeals to the monarch to preserve "his own unborrowed vertue" in politics, but he does not completely rely on the moral sense of the Crown; he takes a tough stance toward arbitrary rule at the same time:

Our *Trimmer* [. . .] professeth solemnly, that were it in his power to chuse, he had rather have his Ambition bounded, by the commands of a wise and Great Master, than let it range with a popular License, Though crowned with successe: Yet he cannot commit such a Sin against that Glorious thing called Liberty, or let his soul stoop so much below it selfe, as to be content, without repining, to have his Reason intirely subdued, or the priviledge of acting like a sencible Creature torn from him, by the Imperious dictates of unlimited Authoritie, in what hand so ever it happeneth to be placed. (239–40)

Halifax admits that people will obey a "wise and Great" king and restrain their "Ambition" from falling into licentiousness, but there is no guarantee that they always have a good monarch in any age. With pragmatic eyes worthy of an experienced statesman, he points out the possibility that a despotic ruler might appear and abuse his "unlimited Authoritie." He unveils his concern about the inconstancy of the human mind and advocates the necessity of law to check the excessive use of the king's power:

But since for the greater honour of good and wise Princes, and the better to set off their Character by the Comparison, Heaven hath decreed there must be a mixture, and that such as are perverse and insufficient, or perhaps both, are at least to have their equall Turns in the Government of the World; and besides that, the will of a man is so various, and so unbounded a thing, and so fatall too, when joyned with power misaplyed; it is no wonder if those who are to be governed are unwilling to have so dangerous as well as so uncertaine a standard of their Obedience. There must be therefore, Rules and Laws [. . .].

There is a wantoness in too great Power that men are generally apt to be corrupted with; and for that Reason a wise Prince, to prevent the temptations arising from common frailty, would chuse to govern by rules for his own Sake, as well as for his people's, since it only secureth him from Errours, and doth not lessen the reall authority that a good magistrate would care to be possessed of. For if the will of a Prince is contrary either to reason it selfe, or to the universall Opinion of his subjects, The Law by a Kind restraint rescueth him from a disease that would undo him; if his will, on the other side, is reasonable and well directed, that Will immediately becometh a Law, and he is Arbitrary by an easie and naturall consequence, without taking paines or overturning the world for it. (186–87)

There is very little room for adopting a genuine republican form of government in his down-to-earth political thought. Again Halifax shows his assent to monarchy: he approves of an autonomous exercise of the power of the magistrate if his will is "reasonable and well directed." His reference to "common frailty" indicates that to err is human, but (to him) not necessarily divine to forgive. God is likely to send bad princes, "perverse" and/or "insufficient" to rule, and the subjects, obliged to obey the ruler whose will might be so "various" and "unbounded," are often exposed to the danger of the political power "misaplyed." The king's power, therefore, must be limited under law which will work as "a Kind restraint," in case the king commits "Errours" that no one can avoid making.

Accordingly, Halifax advocates the role of parliament "because it is an essentiall part of the Constitution" (*Character* 198). It may function as a brake on the Crown's oppression as well as law may, and he takes the consent of the people into account:

> Our *Trimmer* is a freind to Parliaments, notwithstanding all their faults and excesses [. . .]. He thinketh that though they may at some times be troublesome to Authoritie, yet they ad the greatest strength to it under a wise administration. [. . .] Now this cannot be attained by force upon the people, let it be never so great; there must be their Consent too, or else a nation mooveth only by being driven, a sluggish and constrained motion, void of that life and vigour which is necessary to produce great things. Whereas the virtuall Consent of the whole being included in their Representatives, and the King giving the sanction to the united sence of the people, every Act done by such an Authority seemeth to be an effect of their choice, as well as a part of their Duty; and they do with an eagerness, of which men are uncapable whilst under a force, execute what ever is so injoyned as their own will better explained by Parliament, rather than from the terrour of incurring the penalty of the Law for omitting it. (196–97)

Halifax describes the power of parliament as "Politicall Omnipotence" (197). He "beleaveth no Government is perfect except a kind of omnipotence reside in it, to be exerted upon great occasions" (196). Yet it is worth noting that "the virtuall Consent of the whole" must be acknowledged by "their Representatives," and it is the king who finally gives "the sanction to the united sence of the people." The influence of parliament can never be incompatible with the supreme power of the Crown. He adds:

> Our *Trimmer* [. . .] would have had one [a Parliament], because nothing else can unite and heale us; all other means are meere shifts and projects, houses of Cards blown downe with the least breath, and that cannot resist the difficulties which are ever to be presumed [. . .]. And he would have had one, because it might have done the King good, and could not possibly have done him hurt without his owne Consent, which in that Case is not to be Supposed. (198)

Parliament is expected to unite the nation, but Halifax confirms that it should serve for the good of the king in principle. His chief focus is on how the king exercises his power and how to control it in government, and never does he clearly demonstrate his interest in the actual (and future) state of democracy.

Though written briefly, Halifax's elusive but most important political concept in the *Character* is supposed to be "a naturall reason of State":

> When all is said, there is a naturall reason of State, an undefinable thing grounded upon the Common good of mankind, which is immortall, and in all changes and Revolutions still preserveth its Originall right of saving a Nation, when the Letter of the Law perhaps would destroy it; and by whatsoever meanes it moveth carryeth a power with it that admitteth no opposition, being supported by Nature, which inspireth an immediate Consent at some Criticall times into every individuall member, to that which visibly tendeth to the preservation of the whole; and this being so, a wise Prince, instead of controverting the right of this reason of

state, will by all meanes endeavour it may ever be of his side, and then he will be secure. (191)

This passage may tell us his "undefinable" dynamics of law and parliament. Laws are regarded as changeable: even if "the Letter of the Law" misguided the nation, the "naturall reason of State" would correct its course through winning "an immediate Consent" from "every individuall member." Although, based on the analysis so far, it seems unlikely that this "member" includes the populace in Halifax's mind, it is parliament — which he calls "Politicall Omnipotence" (197) — that gains the consent to lay down the policy of the nation. He further insists that "even without the Law," parliament can be "the only provision in extraordinary cases, in which there would be otherwise no Remedie" (198). The king can take counsel with and obtain the support from parliament, which can help him make laws and handle a national emergency where existing laws might fail to do it promptly and properly. It is inferred from his roundabout choice of words that his "naturall reason of State" would mean the political coordinating function of parliament that embraces the sovereignty of the monarch.

It seems also reasonable to suppose that Halifax takes social "changes" and "Revolutions" to be dangerous to the country, and what he pursues most in politics is "the *preservation* of the whole": he is disposed to the maintenance of social order, not the natural rights of the people (*Character* 191; emphasis added). Generally he gives the appearance of claiming that the fair balance should be held between "dominion and Liberty" (194), but actually he does not shift his focus to the subjects so much: whether consciously or unconsciously, his concept of political constitution puts the Crown at the center of government, with parliament as a flexible buffer regulating its discretion. His ideal national polity could be labeled a limited monarchy, with a tendency to a moderate oligarchy which grants lesser power to the masses.

Halifax's political "theory" does not look so systematic as that of his contemporaries, such as the Earl of Clarendon, Thomas Hobbes, and John Locke (1632–1704) (Kenyon, Introduction 31; Quinton 37). His proportioned constitutional eclecticism between absolute monarchy and republicanism, however, unwittingly takes on a tinge of solid conservatism to protect the fundamental structure of the English nation. He modestly inspires patriotism in the *Character*:

> Our *Trimmer* is far from Idolatry in other things, in one thing only he cometh somewhat neere it; his country is in some degree his Idoll: he doth not worship the Sunn, because it is not peculiar to us, it rambleth about the world and is lesse kind to us than it is to other Countries; but for the earth of *England*, though perhaps inferiour to that of many places abroad, to him there is divinitie in it, and he had rather dye than see a spire of English grasse trampled upon by a forreign Trespasser. (237)

It is no doubt that Halifax was definitely conscious of defending his own country from "a forreign Trespasser" — especially France, since Charles II, whose brother was a fervent Catholic, concluded the Secret Treaty of Dover with Louis XIV (1638–1715; r. 1643–1715) in 1670, according to which Charles issued the Declaration of Indulgence to release the Catholics in 1672. From what has been discussed above, we should recognize that the "Trimmer" does not stand genuinely neutral: even if he tries to do so, the Trimmer has a clear bias to a conservative political stance. Moreover, there is a certain validity in saying that, for a trimmer, his professed neutrality is rather an active choice of conservatism than a mere compromise between political extremes. Although his opinions were so unique that he was isolated in contemporary political circles (Kenyon, Introduction 20; Reed 67), Halifax the

Trimmer may have opened the way for dodging radical ideologies to preserve the nation as a whole. Now that his flexibility (both in a good and bad sense) toward party politics with a conservative mindset deserves to be seen as parallel to Swift's would-be disinterested politics, we should examine the political and ideological background of the theory of the ancient constitution to track the historical position of these "trimmers."

3. The Concept of the Ancient Constitution and English Mixed Monarchy

In the seventeenth century, England faced two major crises concerning its form of government: the Civil War and the Glorious Revolution. Both of them threatened the maintenance of the Anglican monarchical system and invited the doom of the reigning sovereign. The former resulted in the execution of Charles I, which led the kingdom to a temporary Puritan republic; the latter was caused by the despotic actions of the Catholic king, James II, which incurred his forced abdication. As is generally known, the country eventually overcame those critical moments and preserved kingship to this day, but its governmental structure did not assume a "pure" form. The English polity can be seen as a mixed constitution, and in view of the contemporary drift of political thought, it is considered likely that the theory of mixed monarchy in no small measure produced the political and constitutional stability in the settlement after the Glorious Revolution.

In the late Stuart period, mixed monarchy was thought to reflect the tradition of the English "ancient constitution." As H. T. Dickinson explains, it indicates that "the supreme authority in the kingdom was the legislature of King, Lords and Commons" (63). Historically, England had abhorred the absolute power of the Crown, even since before the Norman Conquest (1066), and Magna Carta (1215) can be viewed as the symbol of the "success" and the "right" of English subjects (64), thanks to their efforts to "[resist] the actions of their kings" and "[secure] concessions which acknowledged their own liberties" (62). On the grounds of this perception of history, the concept of the ancient constitution was utilized by moderate Tories, who upheld monarchy but despised the absolutism of James II, as well as by the Whigs, who basically laid great store on parliament (27, 62–65). Glenn Burgess argues that the "basic elements" of the ancient constitution are "*custom, continuity,* and *balance*" (*Politics* 4), and it is supposed to keep the equilibrium between the royal prerogative and the liberty of the people (5–6). Unlike that of France, the ancient constitution of England was not developed "as a form of resistance theory" (18), but was concerned "more with explaining how the present [. . .] was to be justified, and why it was to be accepted" (17). The concept "took shape during the late sixteenth century" to defend "the established polity" of the Elizabethan era, inspired by the via media spirit of Richard Hooker in *Of the Laws of Ecclesiastical Polity* (1593–1661) (18, 104).[14] By virtue of this practical sense of balance of power, the idea of mixed monarchy was highly qualified for preventing the total overthrow of the constitution by the Glorious Revolution, maintaining monarchy, and improving the status of parliament at the same time.

In order to unravel the effect of the theory of mixed government underlying the Revolution settlement, Charles I's *His Majesties Answer to the Nineteen Propositions of Both Houses of Parliament* (18 June 1642) can be regarded as "[t]he cardinal document" (Weston 5). In the 1960s, Corinne Comstock Weston cast a spotlight on this *Answer* in *English Constitutional Theory and the House of Lords, 1556–1832,* on the heels of which, in Japan, Daizen Kawamura reacted and left us a valuable examination on it. Both of them pointed out that the *Answer* must have served as a foundation for the Bill of Rights (1689), along with John Locke's *The Two Treatises of Government* (1689) (Kawamura 20; Weston 123). In the 1970s, Dickinson referred to the impact of the *Answer* in his authoritative *Liberty and Property: Political Ideology in Eighteenth-Century Britain* (64–65); in the 1980s, J. G. A. Pocock expressed a particular interest in the *Answer* and Weston's analysis in his noted *The Ancient Constitution and the Feudal Law: A Study of English Historical Thought in the Seventeenth Century* (reissued edition with "A Retrospect from 1986") (308–13). Around the turn of the twenty-first century, however, the significance of the *Answer* seems to be downplayed: for instance, Burgess, who was obviously influenced by Pocock's work and dealt with the concept of the ancient constitution in the Stuart period, gave no due consideration on the *Answer* in *The Politics of the Ancient Constitution: An Introduction to English Political Thought, 1603–1642* and *Absolute Monarchy and the Stuart Constitution*. Based on this premise, we need to attempt a reassessment of the *Answer*, with a comparison to its direct trigger, *Nineteen Propositions* (1 June 1642), which even Weston and Kawamura lacked in their observations. In doing so, we will find how ingeniously (and also accidentally) the Royalist and Parliamentarian causes were blended into the *Answer* to steer a "conservative" middle course in the heat of contemporary and future ideological struggles. This will foster our understanding of the political relevance of Halifax's and Swift's ideas to the history of conservative thought.

"Emboldened by the king's continued weakness" in political strife right before the outbreak of the Civil War, the Long Parliament presented to Charles I the *Nineteen Propositions*, which requested almost "unconditional surrender" from him (Kenyon, *Stuart Constitution* 182). Their demands were "outrageous" or nearly humiliating to him (Greenberg 194), as contrasted with the surroundings of his father, James I (1566–1625; r. 1603–25), who espoused the theory of the divine right of kings. First of all, the king's power to appoint various personnel is expected to be abandoned. In the first proposition, it is declared that Privy Councilors and "great officers and ministers of state, either at home or beyond the seas" must be fully "approved of by both Houses of Parliament" (*NP* 223). The nineteenth proposition even offers to divest the king of his peculiar right to confer a peerage (225). In addition, the "government," "education," and "marriage" of the king's children are to come under the control of parliament (224; props. 4, 5). As for political affairs, the king must follow the Militia Ordinance (Mar. 1642) "made by the Lords and Commons," which did not receive the royal assent because it would make him give up the command of the militia (224; prop. 9). Furthermore, the king's "extraordinary guards and military forces" must be "removed, and discharged," and he cannot raise such forces at will anymore (225; prop. 16). In respect to religion, the king is desired to make "such a reformation" — probably favorable to Presbyterians and Independents — "of the Church government and liturgy, as both Houses of Parliament shall advise" (224; prop. 8). Piling up all these requests, the Parliament ends the *Nineteen Propositions* with a passage that looks like a silent threat as if it tightly holds the purse strings of the king:

> [T]hese our humble desires being granted by your Majesty, we shall forthwith apply ourselves to regulate your present revenue in such sort as may be for your best advantage; and likewise to settle such an ordinary and constant increase of it, as shall be sufficient to support your royal dignity in honour and plenty, beyond [t]he proportion of any former grants of the subjects of this kingdom to your Majesty's royal predecessors. (225–26)

It is no wonder that the acceptance of the *Nineteen Propositions* would lead to the almost total deprivation of the royal authority and an obvious subordination of the Crown to the two Houses. Thus Charles's *Answer* had to be made out as a countermeasure against excessive encroachment by the Parliament.

Now we will take a close look at the *Answer*, focusing on its "all-important discourse on the English constitution" (Weston 123). Of course its key feature is that it boldly announces the political system of England as being made up of a mixed constitution:

> There being three kindes of Government amongst men, Absolute Monarchy, Aristocracy and Democracy, and all these having their particular conveniences and inconveniences, the experience and wisdom of your Ancestors hath so moulded this out of a mixture of these, as to give to this Kingdom [. . .] the conveniences of all three, without the inconveniences of any one, as long as the Balance hangs even between the three Estates [. . .]. (*ANP* 263)

Also highly notable is that the *Answer* clearly distinguishes the political function between the three parts of the government:

> In this Kingdom the Laws are joyntly made by a King, by a House of Peers, and by a House of Commons chosen by the People, all having free Votes and particular Priviledges: The Government according to these Laws is trusted to the King; Power of Treaties of War and Peace, of making Peers, of chusing Officers and Councellours for State, Judges for Law, Commanders for Forts and Castles, giving Commissions for raising men to make War abroad, or to prevent or provide against Invasions or Insurrections at home, benefit of Confiscations, power of pardoning, and some more of the like kinde are placed in the King. [. . .] [T]he House of Commons (an excellent Conserver of Liberty, but never intended for any share in Government, or the chusing of them that should govern) is solely intrusted with the first Propositions concerning the Leavies of Moneys (which is the sinews as well of Peace as

War) and the impeaching of those, who for their own ends, though countenanced by any surreptitiously gotten Command of the King, have violated that Law, which he is bound (when he knows it) to protect, and to the protection of which they were bound to advise him, at least not to serve him in the Contrary. And the Lords being trusted with a Judicatorie power, are an excellent Screen and Bank between the Prince and People, to assist each against any Incroachments of the other, and by just Judgements to preserve that Law, which ought to be the Rule of every one of the three. . . . (263–64)

King, Lords, and Commons respectively reflect the workings of "Absolute Monarchy, Aristocracy and Democracy" (263). The king, for instance, can settle diplomatic problems, equip personnel in his own way, and create peers, as well as summon and dissolve parliament. Even in this brief passage, the *Answer* consciously condenses its response and resistance to the demands of the *Nineteen Propositions* (*NP*, props. 1, 9, 14, 15, 16, 19) in order to advocate a wide range of king's rights. On the other hand, the Lords can hold judicial power, and the Commons the powers of taxation and impeachment (Weston 2). Although the *Answer* defines the English constitution as mixed and "regulated *Monarchy*" to protect kingship (*ANP* 263; emphasis added), it officially degrades the status of the monarch to just one of the three estates because of dividing the power of the government point-blank and proclaiming that "the Balance hangs even between the three Estates." As a result, the theory of the divine right of kings was considered to have been discarded publicly. For Parliamentarians, if the three estates are treated as being "*coordinate* or *concurrent*" (Weston 30), the king can be "outnumbered two to one" (Greenberg 195), so this is regarded as "the great *lapsus calami*" of the *Answer* (Pocock 309). In fact, one of the advisors of Charles I, Edward Hyde, Earl of Clarendon, had been afraid of this degradation of the king. In his eyes, the three estates were essentially composed of the Lords Spiritual, the Lords Temporal, and the Commons; the king was placed as the supreme head of all.[15] Hence it must be admitted that despite the supposed intention of Charles and the Royalists to defend the position and dignity of the Crown, the *Answer* came to give a theoretical advantage to Parliamentarians.

However, we need to pay more attention to the conservative quality of the *Answer*. As a matter of fact, it traces the influence of the classical constitutional theory by Polybius, which can be viewed as an archetype of the theory of mixed government in early modern England.[16] In book 6 of *The Histories*, where he ascribes the cause of Roman dominance to its national polity, Polybius writes:

> Most of those whose object it has been to instruct us methodically concerning such matters [e.g., distinctive qualities of the Roman constitution], distinguishes three kinds of constitutions, which they call kingship, aristocracy, and democracy. Now we should, I think, be quite justified in asking them to enlighten us as to whether they represent these three to be the sole varieties or rather to be the best; for in either case my opinion is that they are wrong. For it is evident that we must regard as the best constitution a combination of all three varieties, since we have had proof of this not only theoretically but by actual experience, Lycurgus having been the first to draw up a constitution — that of Sparta — on this principle. (297; 3.5–8)

> Such being the power that each part has of hampering the others or cooperating with them, their union is adequate to all emergencies, so that it is impossible to find a better political system than this. (345; 18.1)

Polybius pins his hope on "a check and balance system" of this "mixture of monarchy, aristocracy, and democracy" (Weston 11). Without such regulating function, each of the simple or pure forms of government would be corrupted into tyranny, oligarchy, and mobocracy (Polybius 297, 299; 3.9–4.6). It seems reasonable to say that the *Answer* implicitly adapts the rhetoric of Polybius to restrain the anticipated abuse of power by the two Houses.[17] The *Answer* actually warns against granting too much power to parliament:

> [T]he Power Legally placed in both Houses is more then suffi-
> cient to prevent and restrain the power of Tyranny, and without
> the power which is now asked from Us We shall not be able to
> discharge that Trust which is the end of Monarchy, since this would
> be a totall Subversion of the Fundamentall Laws, and that excel-
> lent Constitution of this Kingdom, which hath made this Nation
> so many yeers both Famous and Happy to a great degree of Envie
> [. . .]. (*ANP* 264)

For Royalists, the power of parliament is already excessive, and further concession would be conducive to undermining the constitution. The Commons, representing the people, particularly becomes the target of distrust:

> [T]he second Estate would in all probability follow the Fate of the
> first, and [. . .] Jealousies would be soon raised against them, [. . .]
> till (all Power being vested in the House of Commons, and their
> number making them incapable of transacting Affairs of State with
> the necessary Secrecie and expedition; those being retrusted to
> some close Committee) at last the Common people (who in the
> mean time must be flattered, and to whom Licence must be given
> in all their wilde humours, how contrary soever to established

Law, or their own reall Good) [. . .] set up for themselves, call Parity and Independence, Liberty; devour that Estate which had devoured the rest; Destroy all Rights and Proprieties, all distinctions of Families and Merit; And by this means this splendid and excellently distinguished form of Government end in a dark equall Chaos of Confusion [. . .]. (265)

The *Answer* warns that even the power and status of the Lords would be eroded as those of the king if the growth of the Commons is left unchecked. In order to avoid the destruction (rather than to secure the preservation) of the balance of power among the three estates, the *Answer*, therefore, has recourse to the concept of mixed monarchy, which lives up to the tradition of the English ancient constitution. It is true that Charles and the Royalists made a major compromise with Parliamentarians, but they exerted themselves to maintain the conservative values of English politics and to confront and alleviate the radicality of the *Nineteen Propositions*, which had denied outright much of the royal prerogative (Kawamura 8).

In fact, while the *Answer* brought great disadvantages to the Royalist cause, it certainly left conservative traces in subsequent parliamentary claims. *A Political Catechism* (1643), presumed to have been written by Henry Parker (1604–52), was one of the most prevalent and influential reactions from Parliamentarians. The tract gave a far-reaching impact on contemporaries and posterity, replying to the *Answer* by repeatedly borrowing its wording. As for the diffusion of the *Political Catechism*, three editions appeared in the year of its publication, and later it was republished six times between 1679 and 1710 (Weston 37–38). It can be ranked as "a main channel through which the discourse on the constitution in the Answer to the Nineteen Propositions passed into English political thought" and served as "a prime source of the theory of mixed monarchy" in the Glorious Revolution settlement (38).[18] Even though the *Political Catechism* powerfully furthers the cause of Parliamentarians, it acknowledges that the form of government in England is "Regulated and mixt Monarchy" (*PC* 270; Q. 6). It is also worth noting that it depicts the "Excellent" English polity as "the *Ancient*, Equall, Happy, Well-poysed, and never enough Commended Constitution" (270; A. 6; emphasis added). In spite of supporting the liberty of the people rather than the royal power, it idealizes the regime of "Q. Elizabeths dayes" (272; Q. 12, Obs. 1), which brought forth ancient constitutionalism that was developed to defend the status quo governing structure. What should not be ignored is that even Oliver Cromwell, who actually overturned the monarchy, was conservative in politics (though tolerant in religion) and more sympathetic to a mixed monarchy than a republic. The adoption of Protectorate and the succession of his son, Richard Cromwell (1626–1712; Prot. 1658–59), to Protectorship could reflect his inclination to monarchical government. In addition, not only the introduction of a pseudo-triumvirate system of Protector, Council of State, and Parliament, but also his unrewarding attempt to set up the "Other House" or a second chamber which could perform an equivalent function of the House of Lords are emblematic of his affinity to mixed political mechanism (Kawamura 17–19; Weston 54, 61–63, 65–66). To that extent, the tradition of the English ancient constitution was seminal in the stream of political thought, and Charles I's last-ditch nonviolent resistance to militant parliamentarism contained in the officially-declared *Answer* had a measurable effect on settling the principles and system of mixed monarchy in the near future.

Almost contrary to the original will of Charles I, the *Answer* gave a de facto royal sanction to the authority (or, in another sense, the superiority) of parliament. At the same time, however, it provided, probably in an unexpected fashion, an official conservative alternative to absolute monarchism so as to preserve the regal government of England, that is, the theory of mixed monarchy. Amidst the turbulence of national crises in the seventeenth century, the *Answer* cleverly fused monarchism with parliamentarism and theoretically supported the political stability of the kingdom. In this respect, the conservative character of the *Answer* should never be underestimated in the history of modern political ideas.

As a matter of fact, at the time of the Glorious Revolution, the theory of mixed monarchy was advocated by Halifax, who played the role of the agent to help the escape of James II and the invitation of William of Orange. In the *Character*, the purpose of which was to make a direct appeal to Charles II, Halifax made no particular reference to the *Answer*. It seems unnatural, however, to assume that Halifax was incognizant of his father, Charles I, because Halifax consistently feared, and tried to avoid, the recurrence of civil wars. Instead, in the light of the prevalence of ancient constitutionalism and the *Answer*,[19] we may safely say that his argument could not run away from the influence of the *Answer*. Intentionally or unintentionally, Halifax could convert his ideas into action and manage to maintain the mixed monarchical polity twice: his efforts as a rare nonpartisan fixer culminated in averting the Exclusion Crisis and arbitrating the Revolution settlement.

Let us now return to the assessment of Swift's *Discourse*, where the major characteristics of his views of the state (i.e., the advocacy of mixed government and the power of the monarch, the distrust of the masses, the aversion to the Puritan Revolution and the Catholic kings) bear a striking resemblance to those of Halifax's in the *Character*. Even though there was no mention of Halifax in the *Discourse*, the rhetoric and the persuasive techniques of Swift's political discourse clearly have its basis in the concept of the ancient constitution. In order to construct his argument, Swift refers to Polybius, glamorizes the reign of Elizabeth, and declares his preference for the preservation of social order in revolutionary crises. His fundamental principles of government are significantly in accord with the conservative tradition of English political thought, and the *Discourse* is worth more attention to reveal that it forms the backbone of his politics, regardless of which party is ruling.

Chapter 2

Swift's Views on Church and State
A Tale of a Tub and His Early Religious Works

1. Swift's Animosity against Nonconforming Faith and the Anti-Jacobite Tone in *A Tale of a Tub*

A Tale of a Tub is thought to be the work that almost definitely praises Martin, who embodies Anglicanism. Although it has some satirical tone even to the Anglican via media "strategy of ecclesiastical politics" (Higgins, *Swift's Politics* 135), Swift depicts him as a moderate and prescriptive character. On the other hand, in the eyes of Ian Higgins, Swift lumps Peter (Catholicism) and Jack (Dissent) together and satirizes them as if they are congeneric corrupt nonconformists who threaten the Anglican faith (*Swift's Politics* 41, 106–07, 109–10). Jack "bear[s] a huge Personal Resemblance with his Brother *Peter*": not only "[t]heir Humours and Dispositions," but also "their Shape, their Size and their Mien" are alike enough "for a Bayliff to seize *Jack* by the Shoulders, and cry, *Mr*. Peter, *You are the King's Prisoner*" (*Tale*, *PW* 1: 127; sec. 11). Referring to the historical fact that James II attempted to gain Whig Dissenters over to his side by toleration maneuvers (Higgins, *Swift's Politics* 110), Higgins points out that this type of Swift's rhetoric is in sync with a High-Church allegation of the "political likeness of popery and Dissent" (109).

Indeed Higgins's argument is convincing on the basis of the critical scrutiny of various contemporary discourses and the diligent observation of the trend of opinions in the literary arena at the time, but we should not forget that one of the important aims of the *Tale* is to ridicule Thomas Hobbes. Swift mocks *Leviathan* and warns against the permeation of its influence:

> Sea-men have a Custom when they meet a *Whale*, to fling him out
> an empty *Tub*, by way of Amusement, to divert him from laying
> violent Hands upon the Ship. This Parable was immediately
> mythologiz'd: The *Whale* was interpreted to be *Hobbes*'s *Leviathan*,
> which tosses and plays with all other Schemes of Religion and
> Government, whereof a great many are hollow, and dry, and empty,
> and noisy, and wooden, and given to Rotation. This is the *Leviathan*
> from whence the terrible Wits of our Age are said to borrow their
> Weapons. The *Ship* is in danger, is easily understood to be its old
> Antitype the *Commonwealth*. But, how to analyze the *Tub*, was a
> Matter of difficulty; when after long Enquiry and Debate, the
> literal Meaning was preserved: And it was decreed, that in order to
> prevent these *Leviathans* from tossing and sporting with the
> *Commonwealth*, (which of it self is too apt to *fluctuate*) they should
> be diverted from that Game by a *Tale of a Tub*. (*Tale*, *PW* 1: 24–25;
> preface)

Swift suggests that Hobbes's ideas on government in *Leviathan* would
harm the ship of state, and practically declares that he writes the *Tale* in
order to prevent their adverse effect.[1] Higgins's analysis seems to
overlook a subtle but significant influence of Hobbes on Swift's vision
of church and state.

With this in mind, Swift's juxtaposition of Catholicism and Dissent
in the *Tale* appears comparable to the religious philosophy of Hobbes.
While Hobbes devotes an extensive space of the last two parts of
Leviathan (which deal with the matter of religion) to the criticism
against papism, he briefly reproaches Presbyterianism as a pair of
nonconformity. He complains that the ringleaders of the "Darknesse in
Religion, are the Romane, and the Presbyterian Clergy" (476; pt. 4, ch.

47), and blames the latter for maintaining a false doctrine "*first taught by the Church of Rome*" (475). If we take into account the satirical purpose of the *Tale*, Swift may have deliberately mimicked Hobbes's description of the association between papists and Presbyterians. In this regard, it has to be noted that *Leviathan* was suspected of vindicating Independents, who joined hands with Oliver Cromwell, won the English Civil War, and finally excluded Presbyterians from the Long Parliament. Swift, adherent of the Anglican Church and monarchical constitution, is actually critical of the Puritan Revolution. As mentioned in chapter 1, section 1, in *A Discourse of the Contests and Dissensions in Athens and Rome*, he characterizes Cromwell's seizure of power as "a popular Usurpation" (*PW* 1: 231; ch. 5). On top of that, in the *Tale*, he gives a contemptuous depiction to Jack as follows:

> When he had some Roguish Trick to play, he would down with his Knees, up with his Eyes, and fall to Prayers, tho' in the midst of the Kennel. Then it was that those who understood his Pranks, would be sure to get far enough out of his Way; And whenever Curiosity attracted Strangers to Laugh, or to Listen; he would of a sudden, with one Hand out with his *Gear*, and piss full in their Eyes, and with the other, all to bespatter them with Mud.
>
> In Winter he went always loose and unbuttoned, and clad as thin as possible, to let *in* the ambient Heat; and in Summer, lapt himself close and thick to keep it *out*.
>
> In all Revolutions of Government, he would make his Court for the Office of *Hangman* General; and in the Exercise of that Dignity, wherein he was very dextrous, would make use of no other *Vizard* than a long *Prayer*. (*PW* 1: 124–25; sec. 11)

As commented in the original notes, this passage jeers at "Cromwell *and his Confederates*" (125), presented in the guise of "*Enthusiasts and*

Phanaticks" (124). The hangman's "Exercise of that Dignity" ironically symbolizes the execution of Charles I. The point is that Swift perhaps intentionally mixes up Presbyterians and Independents (and also other sects) when he molds the character of Jack. Judging from his open hostility toward Hobbes, Cromwell, and Independency, this cynical confusion could uncover Swift's designs to lampoon the religious disorder developed in the Great Rebellion and the apparent sectarian indifference of *Leviathan*.[2]

As for the proportion of the blame for nonconforming, Higgins argues that Swift "has the most intense animus" against Dissenting Jack as the "contemporary political threat is perceived to come principally from Dissent not popery" (*Swift's Politics* 117). However, we may become unconvinced that Swift's censure on Roman Catholicism is milder than on Dissent, if we consider the fact that this Anglo-Irish Anglican cleric came from Ireland, where Catholics were overwhelmingly dominant in number (though never in power) and Anglicans were totally in the minority even within Protestants, in spite of the Church of Ireland having its status as the state church. Instead, we can recognize his deep-seated wariness toward papism. At an earlier stage of the *Tale*, Martin and Jack, both symbolizing Protestantism, decide to split with Peter, who "grew so scandalous" as to "by main Force, [. . .] [kick] them both out of Doors," and "never let them come under his Roof," accompanied by "a File of Dragoons," which indicates "*the Civil Power*" of Catholic lords "*employ'd against the Reformers*" (*PW* 1: 75–76; sec. 4). This initial "open Rupture" between the brothers could imply Swift's intent to prescind papists from Protestants in the first place (83; sec. 6). Although Jack later flings "a Million of Scurrilities" at, and produces "a mortal Breach" with, Martin (88), his "Hatred and Spight" against Peter surpass "any Regards after his Father's Commands," and lead him into the condition of Dissenting "*Zeal*" (86). In this sense, Catholicism can be interpreted as a strong incitement to religious conflict that might make Dissenters worse-disposed. As already stated in the previous chapter, Swift implicitly scoffs at the Catholic kings, Charles II and James II, as "two weak Princes" in the *Discourse* (*PW* 1: 230; ch. 5), both of whom repeatedly issued the Declarations of Indulgence (1662, 1672, 1687, 1688) that could allow some liberty of conscience even to Dissenters. In the light of his consistent vigilance against the popish (and French) threat, it is hard to regard Swift as a genuine Jacobite. His aversion to Catholicism is at least as intense as, if not more intense than, that to Dissent.

In fact, Swift accepts the settlement of the Glorious Revolution dethroning James, albeit he seems to breed discontent also with William III's toleration of Dissenters. In the *Discourse*, Swift describes Charles and James as endangering the power balance of the mixed constitution of Britain and values the Revolution because it "very seasonably" prevented their designs to subvert the state (*PW* 1: 230; ch. 5). We should now be reminded that Swift upholds the theory of mixed monarchy: he can never display sympathy with the despotism of James, even though William was not necessarily a simple advocate of parliament. In the last section of the *Tale*, Peter and Jack, who once broke away, conspire to "trepan" Martin and "strip him to the Skin." This indicates James's "*Invitation*" to Presbyterians for being in league with papists and also his exercise of the dispensing power to give "*Liberty of Conscience, which both Papists and Presbyterians made use of,*" in order to stand against the Established Church (*PW* 1: 131; sec. 11). Thankfully, however, their plot is (perhaps "very seasonably" [*Discourse*, *PW* 1: 230; ch. 5]) defeated: Martin "with much ado, shew'd them both a fair pair of Heels." In this scene, Swift elaborately alludes to the hustle and bustle of the Revolution which resulted in the preservation of the mixed monarchy and the Anglican Church system (*Tale*, *PW* 1: 131; sec. 11). In other words, he makes the positive assessment of the post-Revolution national framework, which means that he implicitly (or rather explicitly) shows his approval of the expulsion of James from the throne.

Thus considering his tenacious enmity against Catholicism and James, it seems fairly unreasonable that we define Swift as a Jacobite. To proceed with the discussion on the firmness of his Anglican faith and his anti-Jacobite sentiment, we need to examine his views on religion in the vortex of party and sectarian conflict early in the eighteenth century.

2. Swift's Religious Outlook: Pamphlets during the Years around His Party Conversion

In 1708, when Robert Harley left the Godolphin ministry and went into opposition, Swift wrote *The Sentiments of a Church-of-England Man, with Respect to Religion and Government*, which Higgins sees as "Swift's position statement [. . .] on religion and government" ("Jonathan Swift's Political Confession" 10). According to Herbert Davis, in spite of still (at least nominally) being in the Whig fold, Swift's views were "much nearer the views of Harley though he did not yet know him, than of his 'great friends' among the Whigs; like Harley, he refused to be driven into a purely partisan view and to label himself Whig or Tory." Swift claimed to be "a moderate churchman," and adopted an opposing position against both "the 'low party' of the Dissenters" and "the high Tories, who were either non-jurors or Jacobites" (Introduction, Swift, *PW* 2: xv). It is worthy of attention that *Sentiments* was published in 1711, when Swift completely went over to the Tory side. In view of the time lag between its writing and its publication, as well as of his efforts to steer an apparently middle course, *Sentiments* is a notable work that could subsume his delicate partisan sentiment, which swayed between the two parties and made him balance their conflicting ideologies. Seeking a faithful adherence to Anglicanism and moderate politics, it demonstrates his fundamental ideals of church and state.

The first section of *Sentiments* focuses on the matter of religion. Swift maintains that adherents of the Church of England should pay due respect to the established system of church governance:

> A *Church-of-*England *Man* hath a true Veneration for the Scheme established among us of Ecclesiastical Government; although he will not determine whether Episcopacy be of Divine Right, he is sure it is most agreeable to primitive Institution; fittest, of all others for preserving Order and Purity, and under its present Regulations, best calculated for our Civil State [. . .]. (*PW* 2: 5; sec. 1)

Swift virtually declares that the Anglican Church, run under episcopacy, resembles most closely the ancient ecclesiastical polity and is most suitable for the maintenance of social order. He advocates the unity of church and state: the presence of the state church is of pivotal importance even to secular government. For him, "the Abolishment of this Order among us, would prove a mighty Scandal, and Corruption to our Faith, and manifestly dangerous to our Monarchy" (5). He conditionally approves of the services of different sects, but never admits their further development, which would turn into the threat to the Established Church and also to social stability:

> He [a *Church-of-*England *Man*] is for tolerating such different Forms in religious Worship, as are already admitted; but, by no Means, for leaving it in the Power of those who are tolerated, to advance their own Models upon the Ruin of what is already established; which it is natural for all Sects to desire, [. . .] and yet, which they cannot succeed in, without the utmost Danger to the publick Peace.

> To prevent these Inconveniences, He thinks it highly just, that all Rewards of Trust, Profit, or Dignity, which the State leaves in the Disposal of the Administration, should be given only to those, whose Principles direct them to preserve the Constitution in all its Parts. (6)

This passage hints that the proper functioning of the Anglican Church system is inseparable from the conduct of state affairs. The priority is set on the adequate preservation of the constitution: to that end, Swift upholds intervention by the government to regulate nonconforming movements. On the surface, the wording looks as if toleration in itself is recognized, but he never countenances executing the toleration policy because it can cause damage to the nation at large.

Swift is careful in describing his uncompromising stance on non-Anglican worship. On the one hand, he looks reluctant to support the Occasional Conformity Bill. He shows a sympathetic attitude to those who are against occasional conformity but at the same time against the Bill, because they are concerned that the legal prohibition seems "violent, untimely, and improper." On the other hand, he criticizes their request for "repealing the *Sacramental Test*" as "a little too gross and precipitate." They can make use of the pretext that "no Man should, on the Account of Conscience, be deprived the Liberty of serving his Country," but it will lapse into "[admitting] *Papists, Atheists, Mahometans, Heathens,* and *Jews*" as well as Dissenters (*Sentiments, PW* 2: 6–7; sec. 1). Now it seems unlikely that Swift, declaring himself a "High-churchman" (*Memoirs, PW* 8: 120), connives at occasional conformity: his concessional remarks on it would indicate his deliberate ingratiation with Dissenting Whigs in authority. He would rather avoid extremes of tight regulation and excessive indulgence, and is adamant in putting Anglicanism on the spiritual pillar of the constitution. In fact, he again detests the Puritan Revolution as "the whole Body of

Puritans in *England*" was "drawn to be the Instruments or Abettors of all Manner of Villany, by the Artifices of a *few Men*, whose Designs, from the first, were levelled to destroy the Constitution, both of Religion and Government" (*Sentiments*, *PW* 2: 12; sec. 1). He means to deplore Puritans as indiscreet enough to be used as a tool for what he previously called "a popular Usurpation" by Cromwell and Independents (*Discourse*, *PW* 1: 231; ch. 5). He further states as follows:

[I]t could not easily be forgot, that whatever Opposition was made to the Usurpations of King *James*, proceeded altogether from the Church of *England*, and chiefly from the *Clergy*, and one of the Universities. For, if it were of any Use to recall Matters of Fact, what is more notorious than that Prince's applying himself first to the Church of *England*; and upon their Refusal to fall in with his Measures, making the like Advances to *Dissenters* of all Kinds, who readily and almost universally complied with him; affecting, in their numerous Addresses and Pamphlets, the Style of *Our Brethren the Roman Catholicks*; whose Interests they put on the same Foot with their own: And some of *Cromwell*'s Officers took Posts in the Army raised against the Prince of *Orange*. (*Sentiments*, *PW* 2: 9; sec. 1)

Swift deals with Cromwell and James II en bloc in respect of carrying out "Usurpations." In like manner he also lumps Catholics and Dissenters together as if they conspire to "destroy the Constitution" (12), which can be associated with the collusion between Peter and Jack to entrap Martin in the *Tale*. In doing so, he emphasizes the struggle of the Anglican Church against nonconforming believers and defends the efforts by the former to bring about the Revolution settlement. As a result, Swift's treatment of the rulers and the sectarian strife in the late seventeenth century conveys a negative impression on Jacobite schemes.

The second section of *Sentiments* enters the discussion on government. Swift argues that both parties share a common ground theoretically:

> [D]o not the Generality of *Whigs* and *Tories* among us, profess to agree in the same *Fundamentals*; their Loyalty to the Queen, their Abjuration of the *Pretender*, the Settlement of the Crown in the *Protestant* Line; and a *Revolution Principle*? Their Affection to the Church Established, with Toleration of *Dissenters*? Nay, sometimes they go farther, and pass over into each other's Principles; the *Whigs* become great Asserters of the Prerogative; and the *Tories*, of the People's Liberty; these crying down almost the whole Set of Bishops, and those defending them [. . .]. (*PW* 2: 13–14; sec. 2)

This seems to be Swift's coherent vision of party politics: later in *The Examiner*, even after his conversion to the Tory side, he writes that the Whigs and the Tories "only [. . .] disagree about the Means" (*PW* 3: 13; no. 15, 16 Nov. 1710), not about the principles of national governance (of this more in the next chapter). Whichever party he supports, his basic assumption is that the British political and religious regime is sustained by the security of the Protestant succession and the stability of the Anglican Church. It is necessary to accept the Revolution settlement so as to "preserve the Constitution in all its Parts" (*Sentiments*, *PW* 2: 6; sec. 1), which is his ultimate goal.

In addition to the approbation for the "Abjuration of the *Pretender*" (*Sentiments*, *PW* 2: 13; sec. 2), Swift applies the term "a *weak Prince*" — the epithet previously used in the *Discourse* — to a Catholic king after the Restoration (1660) who "began again to dispose the People to new Attempts; which it was, no doubt, the Clergy's Duty to endeavour to prevent" (17). This *"Prince"* most likely indicates James II, or possibly

Charles II; in any case, he justifies the political choice to dethrone James in the Glorious Revolution:

> As to the *Abdication* of King *James*, which the Advocates on that Side look upon to have been forcible and unjust, and consequently void in it self; I think a Man may observe every Article of the *English* Church, without being in much Pain about it. It is not unlikely that all Doors were laid open for his Departure, and perhaps not without the Privity of the Prince of *Orange*; as reasonably concluding, that the Kingdom might better be settled in his Absence [. . .]. But whether his Removal were caused by his own *Fears*, or other Mens *Artifices*, it is manifest to me, that supposing the Throne to be vacant, which was the Foot the Nation went upon; the Body of the People was thereupon left at Liberty, to chuse what Form of Government they pleased, by themselves, or their Representatives. (20–21)

Swift suggests that James's "Absence" was not a deposition, but an "*Abdication*" which it is the king, not the people or parliament, who is to be blamed for, and which should bring more stability to the kingdom. He seems to stress the function of "king in parliament" even in matters of royal succession as if he derides the promotion of Catholicism and despotism in the reign of James. As we have seen, in his heart Swift wants to preserve mixed monarchy, giving the upper hand to the Crown among the three powers of government. To ensure the legitimacy of the accession of William III, however, he dares to insist on the people's right to "chuse what Form of Government they pleased" to fill up the vacancy of the throne. Notably persistent is his attempt to demonstrate that the abdication of James was an extremely rare situation for the nation:

[A]s our Monarchy is constituted, an Hereditary Right is much to be preferred before *Election*. Because, the Government here, especially by some late Amendments, is so regularly disposed in all its Parts, that it almost executes it self. [. . .] And therefore, this Hereditary Right should be kept so sacred, as never to break the Succession, unless where the preserving it may endanger the Constitution; which is not from any intrinsick Merit, or unalienable Right in a *particular Family*; but to avoid the Consequences that usually attend the Ambition of Competitors, to which elective Kingdoms are exposed [. . .]. Hence appears the Absurdity of that Distinction between a King *de facto*, and one *de jure*, with respect to us: For every *limited* Monarch is a King *de jure*, because he governs by the Consent of the *Whole*; which is the Authority sufficient to abolish all precedent Right. If a King come in by *Conquest*, he is no longer a *limited* Monarch: If he afterwards consent to Limitations, he becomes immediately King *de jure*, for the same Reason. (18–19)

For Swift, the prospective continuation of James's reign would "endanger the Constitution," risky enough to "break the Succession." He intends to illustrate that the Revolution was never a "*Conquest*" by the foreign monarch. Rather, William's crowning was affirmed "by the Consent of the *Whole*," and thus he can be defined as a "*limited* Monarch," (in principle) duly controlled by the parliament. Swift offers a popular excuse for William, the supposed de facto king, becoming the de jure king; to that extent he is negative about taking up the Jacobite cause and champions the Revolution settlement. His argument is consistent in displaying antipathy to, rather than sympathy with, Jacobitism after the *Discourse*.

Now we shall again go back to Swift's inclination to mixed and limited monarchy, which would barely be taken into account in most of the past approaches of Swift studies including Higgins's. Swift maintains:

> Arbitrary Power is but the first natural Step from *Anarchy* or the *Savage Life*; the adjusting *Power* and *Freedom* being an Effect and Consequence of maturer Thinking: And this is no where so duly regulated as in a limited Monarchy: Because I believe it may pass for a Maxim in State, that *the Administration cannot be placed in too* few *Hands*, nor the *Legislature in too* many. Now in this material Point, the Constitution of the *English* Government far exceeds all others at this Time on the Earth; to which the present Establishment of the *Church* doth so happily agree, that I think, whoever is an Enemy to *either*, must of necessity be so to *both*. (*Sentiments*, *PW* 2: 18; sec. 2)

The contrast between "*Power* and *Freedom*" is equivalent to what the Marquess of Halifax counterposes as "dominion and Liberty" in *The Character of a Trimmer* (194): it implies the conflicting relations between the royal authority and civil liberties, or more abstractly, between absolute monarchy and republicanism, which has to be adjusted and "duly regulated" in Britain. Swift clearly intends to seek moderation to steer between extremes. While abhorring the "Arbitrary Power," he vindicates the abundance of the members of parliament. Yet he never wants to grant great power to the people as he also recognizes that the government already has sufficient men in the saddle. To run a sound monarchy, he feels it necessary to maintain the mixed constitution by imposing limitations on the opposing elements. After all, he praises the current Protestant regime and underscores the blending of church and state: moving against the Anglican Church would bring inevitable harm even to the government (*Sentiments*, *PW* 2: 18; sec. 2). As Davis points out that, for Swift, Jacobites look "just as dangerous as the extremists of the low party" of the Dissenters (Introduction, Swift, *PW* 2: xvii), we can acknowledge Swift's adamant conviction that Jacobitism should be set aside along with Dissent to uphold the national polity after the political and sectarian turmoil of the Glorious Revolution.

Written in the same year as *Sentiments*, *An Argument against Abolishing Christianity in England* is deemed a work of irony which Sir Walter Scott (1771–1832) extols as an adequate defense of the Christian faith. Swift's aim is not only to criticize "the whole body of the deists and freethinkers" such as Matthew Tindal (1657–1733) and John Toland (1670–1722), but also to appeal to "his great friends among the Whig leaders [. . .] to recognize the dangers which would result from any attack on the Church of England, as by Law established" (Davis, Introduction, Swift, *PW* 2: xix). Swift sarcastically declares that what he pursues is nominal Christianity, not necessarily real:

> I hope, no Reader imagines me so weak to stand up in the Defence of *real* Christianity; such as used in primitive Times [. . .] to have an Influence upon Mens Belief and Actions: To offer at the Restoring of that, would indeed be a wild Project; it would be to dig up Foundations; to destroy at one Blow *all* the Wit, and *half* the Learning of the Kingdom; to break the entire Frame and Constitution of Things; to ruin Trade, extinguish Arts and Sciences with the Professors of them [. . .].
>
> Therefore, I think this Caution was in it self altogether unnecessary, (which I have inserted only to prevent all Possibility of cavilling) since every candid Reader will easily understand my Discourse to be intended only in Defence of *nominal* Christianity; the other having been for some Time wholly laid aside by general Consent, as utterly inconsistent with our present Schemes of Wealth and Power. (*Argument*, *PW* 2: 27–28)

This seems to be his cynicism toward occasional conformity. Swift, known to be sympathetic to the landed interest and classical values, dares to give a satirical picture of the mercantile tendency of the powers that be, thereby warning the Whigs not to mitigate the Test Act. As Davis analyzes, nominal Christianity is in the main treated as "preferable to open infidelity," and "though he did not hope for real virtue, even the appearance of virtue was better than open vice" (Introduction, Swift, *PW* 2: xix).[3] On first sight, it appears to be a recommendation of hypocrisy, but we need to keep in mind that Swift explains "the Necessity of a *nominal* Religion" to let off steam from non-Anglicans: "Great Wits love to be free with the highest Objects; and if they cannot be allowed a *God* to revile or renounce; they will *speak Evil of Dignities*, abuse the Government, and reflect upon the Ministry; which I am sure, few will deny to be of much more pernicious Consequence" (*Argument*, *PW* 2: 29). Indeed he is more afraid that they would vent their discontent on secular government if they had no chance to reproach an orthodox type of faith, that is, Anglicanism. The other side of the coin, however, is that to such an extent he regards nonconformity — easily calculating on nominal Christianity — as the troubling threat to the security of the Anglican church and state. Judging from his deep sense of crisis against the rise of Dissenting sects, he would rather imply that occasional conformists cannot contribute to the preservation of real Christianity, as he is concerned that it is *their* "Schemes of Wealth and Power" that would readily "break the entire Frame and Constitution of Things" (27–28), which should indicate his ideal national structure, sustained by the Established Church and mixed monarchy.

Swift's intention to uphold the Church of England amounts to almost omnidirectional attack on non-Anglican sects:

[T]he Abolishing of Christianity may perhaps bring the Church in Danger [. . .]. Nothing can be more notorious, than that the *Athe-*

ists, Deists, Socinians, Anti-Trinitarians, and other Subdivisions of Free-Thinkers, are Persons of little Zeal for the present Ecclesiastical Establishment: Their declared Opinion is for repealing the Sacramental Test; they are very indifferent with regard to Ceremonies; nor do they hold the *Jus Divinum* of Episcopacy. Therefore this may be intended as one politick Step towards altering the Constitution of the Church Established, and setting up *Presbytery* in the stead [. . .].

In the last place, I think nothing can be more plain, than [. . .] that the Abolishment of Christian Religion, will be the readiest Course we can take to introduce Popery. And I am the more inclined to this Opinion, because we know it hath been the constant Practice of the *Jesuits* to send over Emissaries, with Instructions to personate themselves Members of the several prevailing Sects amongst us. So it is recorded, that they have at sundry Times appeared in the Guise of *Presbyterians, Anabaptists, Independents,* and *Quakers*, according as any of these were most in Credit: So, since the Fashion hath been taken up of exploding Religion, the *Popish* Missionaries have not been wanting to mix with the Free-Thinkers [. . .]. (*Argument, PW* 2: 36–37)

Given this rooted antipathy to nonconforming, there is very little room for him to accept occasional conformity. Dissenting sects are definitely viewed as enemies of the Established Church, and they are likely to be utilized as camouflage by Catholics, who are regarded as equivalent to "the Evil we chiefly pretend to avoid" (37). The way he brackets Catholics and Dissenters here reminds us of the one in the *Tale*. Such offensive rhetoric about religious toleration would reflect his continued strategy to defend the Revolution settlement.

As regards further reference to the relation of church and state, Swift notes the need for powerful royal prerogative and the virtue of the Crown. In *A Project for the Advancement of Religion, and the Reformation of Manners*,[4] he writes:

> [H]uman Nature seems to lie under this Disadvantage, that the Example alone of a vicious Prince, will in Time corrupt an Age; but the Example of a good one will not be sufficient to reform it without further Endeavours. Princes must therefore supply this Defect by a vigorous Exercise of that Authority, which the Law hath left them, by making it every Man's Interest and Honour to cultivate Religion and Virtue; by rendering Vice a Disgrace, and the certain Ruin to Preferment or Pretensions [. . .]. (*PW* 2: 47)

He attaches higher value to "Religion and Virtue" than to "Capacity and Understanding" in personnel management in government.[5] The monarch is required to exemplify virtue and exert his or her power "without Interposition of the Legislature" to accomplish a "Reformation" in British society (49). In order to prevent "many Corruptions [. . .] in every Branch of Business" which were "almost inconceivable," Swift insists that the only countermeasure is "the Certainty of being hanged upon the first Discovery, by the arbitrary Will of an unlimited Monarch, or his *Vizier*" (58). He goes on to explain:

> What Remedy, therefore, can be found against such Grievances in a Constitution like ours, but to bring Religion into Countenance, and encourage those who, from the Hope of future Reward, and Dread of future Punishment, will be moved to act with Justice and Integrity?
>
> This is not to be accomplished any other Way, than by introducing Religion, as much as possible, to be the Turn and Fashion of the Age; which only lies in the Power of the Administration; the Prince with utmost Strictness regulating the Court, the Ministry,

and other Persons in great Employment; and these, by their Example and Authority, reforming all who have Dependance on them. (58–59)

Swift emphasizes the role of religion to clean up politics. To promote virtue in the British constitution, he calls for secular power and especially puts the royal authority above every other power apparatus. He consistently advocates the current regime and attempts to take a conservative line: "What I principally insist on is the due Execution of the old [Laws], which lies wholly in the Crown, and in the Authority derived from thence" (61).

All in all, Swift's theory of religion is inseparable from his ideals of national polity. He is coherent in adhering to mixed and limited monarchy, giving the utmost importance to the regal power subsequent to the *Discourse*. Based on this political configuration, he sticks to criticize nonconforming sects in block subsequent to the *Tale*. His early religious works speak out against Jacobitism while they may initially aim to reproach any kind of Dissent. To put his principles into practice, he attempts to warn against the promotion of the toleration policy of the Whigs and the excessive support for the Stuart cause by the Tories at the same time. In *Sentiments*, we can recognize his determination on this matter: "I should think that, in order to preserve the Constitution entire in Church and State; whoever hath a true Value for both, would be sure to avoid the Extreams of *Whig* for the Sake of the former, and the Extreams of *Tory* on Account of the latter" (*PW* 2: 25; sec. 2). It is reasonably evident from his statements that his moderate stance to prevent extremes both in politics and religion with a loyalty to the Anglican establishment was formed from the beginning of his political and literary career. Now to foster a deeper understanding of his views on church and state, it would be of valuable help to examine how and why he displays a critical attitude toward Hobbes.

3. Church and State in *Leviathan* and Swift's Antipathy to Hobbes

As we have seen in section 1, Swift releases his hostility to *Leviathan* in the *Tale*. In terms of the political constitution, however, Hobbes and Swift are coincidentally in agreement on the distrust of the people. In spite of its overall tone generally interpreted as a vocal vindication of democracy, we can read *Leviathan* from rather a conservative angle, because Hobbes seems to rate monarchy superior to the other two types of government. Actually, he states:

> [F]or the most part, if the publique interest chance to crosse the private, he [whosoever beareth the Person of the people, or is one of that Assembly that bears it] preferrs the private: for the Passions of men, are commonly more potent than their Reason. From whence it follows, that where the publique and private interest are most closely united, there is the publique most advanced. Now in Monarchy, the private interest is the same with the publique. The riches, power, and honour of a Monarch arise onely from the riches, strength and reputation of his Subjects. For no King can be rich, nor glorious, nor secure; whose Subjects are either poore, or contemptible, or too weak through want, or dissention, to maintain a war against their enemies: Whereas in a Democracy, or Aristocracy, the publique prosperity conferres not so much to the private fortune of one that is corrupt, or ambitious, as doth many times a perfidious advice, a treacherous action, or a Civill warre. (131; pt. 2, ch. 19)

Hobbes points out that human beings, by nature, are apt to act for their own profit because he believes that passions would prevail over reason in ordinary circumstances.[6] Thus he degrades aristocracy and democracy as being much more likely to stir up and spread men's desires for private interest, all the more because they have more than one man in their division of power. In contrast, monarchy is expected to tie the sovereign's private and public interests together and to run a smaller risk of corruption. He further asserts: "There is a [. . .] doctrine, plainly, and directly against the essence of a Common-wealth; and 'tis this, *That the Soveraign Power may be divided.* For what is it to divide the Power of a Common-wealth, but to Dissolve it? for Powers divided mutually destroy each other" (225; pt. 2, ch. 29). Here Hobbes clearly rejects the segmentation of *"the Soveraign Power"* within a nation, as it would lead the country to ruin. He is most probably afraid of civil wars at worst, like the Puritan Revolution, by mutual destruction between the divided powers in pursuit of their own profit. In conjunction with the occasional exposure of his undervaluation on the capacity of the multitude,[7] this purports to show his inclination toward monarchy (the form that is governed by a single sovereign), not the admiration for democracy (Nakajima, "Thomas Hobbes's Advocacy" 23–26). As already noted in chapter 1, Swift also points out that the will of a group is liable to turn into disunion because "[s]o endless and exorbitant are the Desires of Men, whether considered in their Persons or their States, that they will grasp at all, and can form no Scheme of perfect Happiness with less" (*Discourse, PW* 1: 202; ch. 1).

Nonetheless, Swift does not appreciate Hobbes. For one thing, from the viewpoint of Swift, Hobbes's argument appears to be lukewarm in denying the efficacy of democracy and pander to the side of the common people. Certainly Hobbes subordinates democracy, but we might say that he does not dismiss outright the concept of a democratic government. Although Hobbes leans to monarchy to hold the risk of civil wars to a minimum, he can actually be considered to have recognized democracy as *one* of the legitimate modes of governance, along with the other two (Nakajima, "Thomas Hobbes's Advocacy" 33). Another possible, but more decisive, reason would be that Hobbes expresses open skepticism about mixed monarchy:

> Sometimes also in the meerly Civill government, there be more than one Soule: [. . .] This endangereth the Common-wealth, sometimes for want of consent to good Lawes; but most often for want of such Nourishment, as is necessary to Life, and Motion. For although few perceive, that such government, is not government, but division of the Common-wealth into three Factions, and call it mixt Monarchy; yet the truth is, that it is not one independent Common-wealth, but three independent Factions; nor one Representative Person, but three. [. . .] [I]f the King bear the person of the People, and the generall Assembly bear also the person of the People, and another Assembly bear the person of a Part of the people, they are not one Person, nor one Soveraign, but three Persons, and three Soveraigns. (228; pt. 2, ch. 29)

> [A]ll Governments, which men are bound to obey, are Simple, and Absolute. In Monarchy there is but One Man Supreme; [. . .] And in Aristocracy, and Democracy, but One Supreme Assembly, with the same Power that in Monarchy belongeth to the Monarch, which is not a Mixt, but an Absolute Soveraignty. And of the three sorts, which is the best, is not to be disputed, where any one of them is already established; but the present ought alwaies to be preferred, maintained, and accounted best [. . .]. (379; pt. 3, ch. 42)

All types of political constitution must be "Simple, and Absolute," not "Mixt," and Hobbes plainly values the existing governing structure. In the case of England, he most practically acknowledges regal government. Regarding the three parties that might hold the reins of power, "the generall Assembly" would figure democracy, and "another

Assembly" representing "a *Part* of the people" aristocracy (emphasis added). If we apply this to the English monarchical system, it is obvious that the Houses of Commons and Lords would respectively reflect their function. Putting little trust in the innate goodness of human nature, "subject to diversity of opinions" (228; pt. 2, ch. 29), Hobbes shows his deep concern for the split of the body politic caused by setting up such "independent" triangular structure. After all, he deprecates mixed monarchy as factionalism, the result of which he supposes would be a national disaster, plausibly hinting at a civil war[8] (Nakajima, "Thomas Hobbes's Advocacy" 28–29). This is demonstrably irreconcilable with Swift's contention that mixed monarchy will work if the three powers are well-balanced, with a managerial superiority on the part of the king.

As to the religious framework of the country, Hobbes looks positive about the unity of church and state (or rather, the "subordination of the church to the state" [Curley 309]). Below is his definition of the church in *Leviathan*:

> I define a CHURCH to be, *A company of men professing Christian Religion, united in the person of one Soveraign; at whose command they ought to assemble, and without whose authority they ought not to assemble.* And because in all Common-wealths, that Assembly, which is without warrant from the Civill Soveraign, is unlawful; that Church also, which is assembled in any Common-wealth, that hath forbidden them to assemble, is an unlawful Assembly. (321; pt. 3, ch. 39)

On this premise, Hobbes expounds his views on the relation between church and state:

> There is therefore no other Government in this life, neither of State, nor Religion, but Temporall; [. . .] And that Governor must

be one; or else there must needs follow Faction, and Civil war in the Common-wealth, between the *Church* and *State*; between *Spiritualists* and *Temporalists*; between the *Sword of Justice*, and the *Shield of Faith*; and (which is more) in every Christian mans own breast, between the *Christian*, and the *Man*. The Doctors of the Church, are called Pastors; so also are Civill Soveraignes: But if Pastors be not subordinate one to another, so as that there may bee one chief Pastor, men will be taught contrary Doctrines, whereof both may be, and one must be false. Who that one chief Pastor is, according to the law of Nature, hath been already shewn; namely, that it is the Civill Soveraign [. . .]. (322)

Again he is most concerned about the possibility of civil wars, in this case caused by the division of political and religious forces. To avoid domestic turmoil, the monarch must be the "chief Pastor" of the nation, which functions as the symbol of the unity of the spiritual and the secular. Such an endorsement of the royal authority in the realm of ecclesiastical affairs is conducive to supporting the supremacy of the Church of England, as it coincides with "conventional Anglican beliefs" that "a Christian church and state constitute one united body," and "supreme power over the church is in the hands of the head of the state" (Sommerville 363).

At first glance, Hobbes's apparently favorable stance toward the Anglican establishment is compatible with Swift's sectarian loyalty as "*a Church-of-England Man*." However, it should be noted that, as Patricia Springborg indicates, Hobbes professes "a vehement anti-clericalism" as well as "official conformity to the doctrines of the Anglican Church" ("Hobbes" 347). For Hobbes, it is not the clergy, but the sovereign, that can authorize official interpretations of the Bible:

When a difficulty arose, the Apostles and Elders of the Church

66

assembled themselves together, and determined what should bee
preached, and taught, and how they should Interpret the Scriptures
to the People [. . .]. The Apostles sent divers Letters to the Churches,
and other Writings for their instruction; which had been in vain, if
they had not allowed them to Interpret, that is, to consider the
meaning of them. And as it was in the Apostles time, so it must be
till such time as there should be Pastors, that could authorise an
Interpreter, whose Interpretation should generally be stood to: But
that could not be till Kings were Pastors, or Pastors Kings. (355–56;
pt. 3, ch. 42)

He goes on to insist that "the Right of Judging what Doctrines are fit for
Peace, and to be taught the Subjects, is in all Common-wealths
inseparably annexed [. . .] to the Soveraign Power Civill" (372). Due to
his misgivings about the "diversity of opinions" among the people (228;
pt. 2, ch. 29), he would think that "situations of divided loyalty between
God and sovereign are likely to arise" if "each person is responsible for
interpreting God's word" (Finn 113). Thus, by making the king "the
judge of what men should be taught," Hobbes intends to promote "the
alignment of opinion and judgement" to maintain social order of the
commonwealth (Tuck 85). Despite such intentions on his part, according
to Johann Sommerville, "[m]ost Anglicans were not willing to pursue
their theory of the Royal Supremacy to quite this extreme," as "Hobbes
eroded any significant distinction between clergy and laity, thus draining
clerical power of all supernatural elements" (368). In the light of his
"Sentiments" and status as an Anglican clergyman, therefore, Swift
could never accept a considerable anticlerical pressure which Hobbes
proposes, even though Swift favors strong regal power.

There should be no doubt that Swift was fairly influenced by
Leviathan in the process of forming his own concept of national polity.
It can work almost as a negative example: Hobbes's dislike of mixed

constitution and clericalism arguably aroused a sense of opposition in Swift's mind. His firm adherence to the Anglican establishment made him feel obliged to take ideological countermeasures against Hobbesian views of church and state. No less important is the fact that Swift had the real-life experience of the Glorious Revolution, which managed to maintain the ancient constitution, while Hobbes could see only the Puritan Revolution, which was remembered as a traumatic memory of despotic Protectorship and religious Independency for contemporary society. Hence it seems reasonable to suppose that, taking pride in the successful experience of preserving regal government and the Anglican Church, differently from the time of Hobbes, Swift may have competitively upheld Anglicanism and the principle of mixed monarchy with a sarcastic innuendo against him, as typically described in the *Tale*.

Chapter 3

Active Nonpartisanship in Swift's Tory Tracts
The Examiner and *The Conduct of the Allies*

1. The Transformation of Tory and Whig Ideologies

Party ideologies after the Glorious Revolution underwent a subtle and gradual transformation compared to those that originated from the Exclusion Crisis. In the early stages, Toryism is typically associated with monarchism, Anglicanism, and the landed interest, and Whiggism with parliamentarism, Dissent, and the moneyed interest. However, the Revolution, which culminated in the ouster of the current king and the invitation of a foreign one, inescapably required both parties to justify their political position under such state of national emergency: they needed to defend themselves concerning how and why they acknowledged the exceptional replacement of the Crown.

In the first place, as J. R. Western indicates, the possible contemporary meaning of the word "revolution" was "change," especially "of a natural and moderate kind." The Revolution was nominally a bloodless one, at least maintaining the monarchical constitution, and it was the outcome of "avoid[ing] radical change," led by people "at the top of the existing social and political structure." In other words, it was no more than a "*modest* progress [. . .] in securing parliamentary supremacy and individual freedom after 1688" (1–4; emphasis added).

As to the handling of the government, J. H. Plumb focuses on the efficacy and benefit of patronage. Controlling patronage, that is, wielding the authority to appoint and dismiss officials, was the crucial factor in the possession of political power. He contends: "It was patronage that cemented the political system, held it together, and made it an almost impregnable citadel, impervious to defeat, indifferent to social change. [. . .] Place was power; patronage was power; and power is what men in politics are after" (189). The struggle for political power can be identified with the scramble for patronage among the various political factions. Those in power, whether Whig or Tory, had to be transformed into conservatives because they wanted to protect their vested interests in the patronage system. Although the Tories had usually been in opposition, Toryism never disappeared. Even the Whigs, typically in the age of Robert Walpole, 1st Earl of Orford (1676–1745), adopted conservative principles to maintain their influence in political circles. Plumb observes: "The evolution of political stability had gone hand in hand not only with the diminution and close control of the electorate and a more thorough exploitation of patronage, but also with the evolution of single-party government and the proscription of a political opposition" (172). The election system was developed in the first age of party politics. This could be seen as a dawn of democracy, but constituencies, in reality, gradually became privileges limited to men of property because election expenses continually increased (85–86). The populace was not able to substantially enjoy the "liberty" acquired in the Revolution. Politics after the Revolution was not so much characterized by the development of democracy in the modern sense as by a growing success of oligarchy.

According to H. T. Dickinson, Tory ideology was a "theory of order." It upheld five features: "absolute monarchy, divine ordination, indefeasible hereditary succession, non-resistance and passive obedience" (15). The political thought of Sir Robert Filmer (c. 1588–1653) expounded in *Patriarcha* (1680) is in accord with these doctrines. In fact, his patriarchal theory is considered "a good example of ideas which were commonly — though not universally — held by seventeenth-century royalists and Tories" (xxiv). Although Filmer's ideas served as a basis of the Tory ideology due to its thorough conservatism,

Toryism in practice had to be moderated in conformity with the political reality of the Revolution. The accession of the foreign ruler, William III, forced the moderate Tories to compromise some of their principles to ensure their survival. As regards absolute monarchy and its divine ordination, their loyalty to the king shifted to a loyalty to the ancient constitution, that is, the mixed government of Crown, Lords, and Commons, which Filmer had practically repudiated. As for indefeasible hereditary succession, they limited it by refusing to recognize a Catholic monarch who could not fulfill the role of protector of the interests of the Established Church. To maintain their ideology of order after the Revolution, the Tories gave a renewed significance to the last two doctrines, non-resistance and passive obedience, through these transitions (Dickinson 27–29). Actually, they had to give priority to the allegiance to the Anglican Church over the allegiance to the king since they had abandoned James II. Those who could not accept these changes took a hard line and became Jacobites.

The Whigs, long considered the driving force of the Revolution, did not have a monolithic solidarity. The republicans, who ardently upheld the rights of the people, were a minority within the party. Certainly Whig ideology was a "theory of liberty," which advocated "the social contract, the natural rights of man and the ultimate sovereignty of the people," but the Junto, the most influential faction which Sidney Godolphin counted on to maintain a ruling coalition, took a pragmatic attitude in order to seize and keep political power in their government offices. Indeed, the majority of the Whigs were conservative. "Most active Whigs" were men of means, and they "wanted a stable, orderly, even hierarchical society which would protect the privileges and property of the wealthy and influential" by entrusting the political power to "responsible men of their own type." They never hoped "to dismantle the Established Church or to sever all the links between Church and State." As a matter of fact, the Whigs were afraid of "social revolution" by the common subjects because it would threaten the profit and influence of men of property (Dickinson 57). In general, the political theory which John Locke expounded in *Two Treatises of Government* was regarded as the central tenet of the "liberal" Whig ideology (Ashcraft 1), but, as J. P. Kenyon remarks, "[t]he truth is, the constitutional theories put forward by defenders of the Revolution were not really 'Lockean' at all, except for their use of the term 'contract', which in any case was part of the common vocabulary of politics long before Locke appeared on the scene" (*Revolution Principles* 2). Furthermore, Dickinson claims that the Whigs preferred the "concept of an ancient constitution" to the contract theory. The former "placed limits on the power of the English Crown and recognized the privileges and authority of Parliament," but "did not advocate a democratic system of government"; the latter, "as put forward by Locke and Algernon Sidney [1622–83]," held "more radical assumptions about the equality of man, the existence of certain universal and inalienable natural rights, and the ultimate sovereignty of the people" (61–62). The Whigs, neither markedly liberal nor close to the people, were disposed to be defenders of their own oligarchic privileges.

The increasing conservativism of the Whigs and the moderation of the Tories in the late Stuart period caused another intense conflict — between Court and Country — which escalated, particularly in the early Hanoverian age (the reign of the first two Georges).[1] Here we can borrow Dickinson's definition:[2]

> [B]oth parties are often described as alliances of two elements: a 'Court' element of professional politicians who wanted power and were anxious for office, and a larger 'Country' element of natural backbenchers who cared little for office and who could not always be trusted to support the political ambitions of their party leaders. In both parties the pull of office and the desire for power could

persuade some of the more ambitious politicians to put loyalty to the Court above loyalty to the party. At the same time, hostility to what was regarded as the excessive power of the executive and the corrupt tactics of the Court could provoke the Country elements of both parties to form a temporary alliance in order to oppose some particular measure of the Government. (91–92)

The profits of patronage frequently united some of the factions in both parties. For instance, Godolphin and Robert Harley swam with the tide of party strife, controlling the coalition government by distributing places to the members, whether Whig or Tory. Walpole refined this method, cleverly removed enemies, and established the age of the so-called Whig supremacy installed by the "Court" Whigs.[3] The Court interest could easily abandon their original doctrines in the face of the attraction — both the influence and the profit — of patronage. On the other hand, the Country opposition in the age of Walpole consisted of the "Whig malcontents" who were ambitious to hold office, the "radical Whigs or Commonwealthmen" and the Jacobites (both extreme factions but small in number), and the "Tory country gentlemen" who formed the largest part (166). Although in many cases it was lacking in unity and "rarely powerful enough to bring down a Whig administration" because the principles of each group were fundamentally different, it could stand together to resist corruption and work as a deterrent which was "strong enough to inhibit the Court's freedom of manoeuvre" (169).

There should always be a risk of oversimplification when attempting to give a clear-cut definition of each party and faction especially in the late seventeenth to the early eighteenth century, because political groups at the time were subject to constant realignments that could be concurrent with nearly every possible shift in policy, either religious or political. However, to sum up the discussion so far, it seems probable at least that a simple dichotomy between the "conservative" Tories and the "progressive" Whigs had increasingly become less serviceable as an inclusive categorization. Both the Tories and the Whigs after the Glorious Revolution had grown conservative almost at the same rate, each absorbing the principles of the other.[4] This observation suggests that political principles themselves can change in close step with human desire. Swift's supposed indifference to partisanship throughout his political career would indicate that he penetrated deeply into the human motives behind these ideological philosophies.

2. Swift's Views of Party

With such trend of thought in mind, we will now proceed to the investigation of Swift's Tory pamphlets. It needs to be noted that they had a "dual purpose": to manipulate public opinion so as to win votes from the electorate, and to ensure Tory control of parliament by gaining support from the MPs. His employer Harley thought it necessary to appeal to the "nation at large" in order to keep up his middle-of-the-road government, whose power base was not solid enough (Downie, *Robert Harley* 126). Since the Harley administration from the outset counted on the moderate Whigs as well as the Tories, a rhetoric that might save the face of both sides was preferred.[5] Swift was expected to take an impartial stand and avoid extremes. He needed to set a conservative tone that would meet with Tory approval, and at the same time to advance a progressive argument that could win the sympathy of the moderate Whigs.

Swift's "moderation" is, however, highly disputable. Richard I. Cook states that "[t]he face Swift presents in the intermediate *Conduct of the Allies* (1711) is in nearly all respects identical with that of the *Examiner* (1710–11), as he continues to assure his readers of his honesty, impartiality, and, most especially, independence," but he adds reservations to the way Swift pretends to maintain neutrality:

> [T]he "impartiality" so boldly claimed by the *Examiner* is of a special sort. The *Examiner* is no detached observer judiciously standing above the political arena and calmly weighing the virtues and defects of each set of antagonists, for such impartiality implies a certain indifference, and Swift pretends no such lack of commitment. His impartiality is of another and higher sort. Both explicitly and by implication he presents himself as a man of fixed patriotic, religious, and moral principles; a man who has referred to those principles in surveying the political scene and has accordingly given his support to the party which best embodies them. If the author of the *Examiner* finds next to nothing worth praising among the Whigs and still less worth criticizing among the Tories, the reasons are to be found not in any vulgar party bias on his part but rather in his firm conviction as to where political virtue currently lies. Of party affiliations as such, the *Examiner* explains in number 43, he is contemptuous. His allegiance is to individuals and policies of virtue, not to factions of any one label. (38)[6]

For Swift, to support a certain party was not necessarily the end, but rather the means to approach his ideals. Even if we cannot rigorously define his true partisanship, it should be possible to appreciate the political attitudes and principles that he accepted by querying his apparently disinterested contentions.

In order to test Swift's indifference to party division itself, the first step is to look into *The Examiner* no. 43 (31 May 1711), as Cook suggests above. Swift gives his definition of each party as follows:

> Whoever formerly professed himself to approve the *Revolution*, to be against the *Pretender*, to justify the Succession in the House of

Hanover, to think the *British* Monarchy not absolute, but limited by Laws, which the Executive Power could not dispense with; and to allow an Indulgence to scrupulous Consciences; such a Man was content to be called a *Whig*. On the other side, whoever asserted the QUEEN'S Hereditary Right; that the Persons of Princes were Sacred; their lawful Authority not to be resisted on any Pretence; nor even their Usurpations, without the most extream Necessity: That, Breaches in the Succession were highly dangerous; that, *Schism* was a great Evil, both in it self and its Consequences; that, the Ruin of the *Church*, would probably be attended with that of the *State*; that, no Power should be trusted with those who are not of the established Religion; such a Man was usually called a *Tory*. (*PW* 3: 166)

His color-coding of both sides looks fairly clear and innocuous, but, as described in section 1, once coming to power, politicians, regardless of whether they were Whig or Tory, tended to become conservative in order to preserve their vested interests and to take advantage of patronage as much as possible. Accordingly, the ideological borderline between the two parties came to be blurred. For example, Tories upheld the superiority of parliament over the royal prerogative, and Whigs supported the Established Church from fear of a separation of church and state, especially to accept the Revolution settlement. Swift states, with a suspicion of satire:

[L]et any one examine a reasonable honest Man of either Side, upon those Opinions in Religion and Government, which both Parties daily buffet each other about; he shall hardly find one material Point in difference between them. I would be glad to ask a Question about *two Great Men* of the late Ministry [John Churchill, 1st Duke of Marlborough (1650–1722), and Godolphin], how they came to be *Whigs?* And by what figure of Speech, half a Dozen others, lately put into great Employments, can be called *Tories?* I doubt, whoever would suit the Definition to the Persons, must make it directly contrary to what we understood it at the Time of the Revolution. (15; no. 15, 16 Nov. 1710)

W. A. Speck gives us an intelligible account of this point:

> Political propagandists distorted the nature of these differences [of opinion between the parties on major political issues], Whigs by asserting that the Tories were conniving with Popery, Jacobitism, and Louis XIV's aim of world domination, Tories by claiming that the Whigs were a gang of republican, presbyterian war-mongers. In his more ferocious sallies against the Whigs after 1710 Swift himself was quite capable of such wilful misrepresentation. [. . .]
>
> Thinking men, seeing that the reality scarcely squared with these notions, and that the bulk of both parties consisted of Anglicans committed to the Hanoverian settlement, dismissed the propaganda as lies, and concluded that at bottom there was really no difference in principle between Whigs and Tories. Swift in his more moderate writings frequently took this line. ("From Principles to Practice" 74)

Swift declares that the difference, if any, between the parties is just that of their perception of what provokes national crises. For him, the Whigs "apprehend the Danger [. . .] from the *Pretender* and his Party," which would promote French invasion, while the Tories fear "the Violence and Cunning of *other Enemies* to the Constitution," which may possibly indicate the Whigs. The two-party confrontation looks "as if two *Brothers* apprehended their House would be set upon, but disagreed about the Place from whence they thought the *Robbers* would come; and therefore would go on different Sides to defend it," only to "weaken and expose themselves by such a *Separation*." It must be true that, at this stage, working as a Tory pamphleteer under the guidance of Harley, Swift places the "*other Enemies*," or "*another Faction*," as posing more risk to the nation at large than "*Popery* and *Slavery*," which he defines as "without doubt the greatest and most dreadful" danger to the state. However, what should be emphasized is that he treats factional conflict almost on a par with Catholicism as the main fear factor against stable national governance (*Examiner*, *PW* 3: 166–67; no. 43).

Indeed, Swift does not place much confidence in the framework of party politics: "*Parties* do not only split a Nation, but every Individual among them, leaving each but half their Strength, and Wit, and Honesty, and good Nature; but one Eye and Ear, for their Sight and Hearing, and equally lopping the rest of the Senses" (*Examiner*, *PW* 3: 102; no. 31, 8 Mar. 1710–11). In *The Conduct of the Allies*, he plainly asserts that the Whigs are "out of all Credit or Consideration," but with regard to the Tory side, he puts it this way:

> The reigning Favourites had always carried what was called the *Tory Principle*, at least, as high as our Constitution could bear: and most others in great Employments, were wholly in the Church-Interest. These last, among whom several were Persons of the greatest Merit, Quality, and Consequence, were not able to endure the many Instances of Pride, Insolence, Avarice and Ambition, which those Favourites began so early to discover, nor to see them presuming to be the sole Dispensers of the Royal Favour. (*PW* 6: 42)

Swift approves of applying the "*Tory Principle*," but adds subtle restrictive notes: "what was called," "at least," and "as high as our Constitution could bear." He never describes the "reigning Favourites" as Tories, still less well-meaning ones, nor declares himself to be a Tory. What he most sympathizes with is probably the "Church-Interest," which can on the whole embrace the Tory backers, but given that he chooses to express the factional composition of the political circles in such a deliberately roundabout way, this could readily allow an implication beyond the two-party system. It can be admitted that though he detested the former Whig government (or rather the Godolphin ministry), he was not exactly eager to give a warm welcome to a pro-Tory one.

In a word, the distinction between Whig and Tory as such counted for little with Swift's politics. Without doubt he was "no detached observer" in the contemporary party strife (Cook 38), but at least he had a strong reluctance to rely on a "dual party system" (Davis, Introduction, Swift, *PW* 3: xiii).

3. British Political Conditions in the Eyes of Swift

Having observed his peculiar nonpartisanship, we shall then look into Swift's judgments on British society after the Glorious Revolution and see what kind of phenomena he deemed the problems of the nation to be. First of all, as was the case with *A Discourse of the Contests and Dissensions in Athens and Rome*, Swift does not regard the Revolution as a civil one in the *Examiner*. If anything, he places its settlement in a conservative line:

> Most of the Nobility and Gentry who invited over the Prince of *Orange*, or attended him in his Expedition, were true Lovers of their Country and its Constitution, in Church and State; and were brought to yield to those Breaches in the Succession of the Crown, out of a Regard to the Necessity of the Kingdom, and the Safety of

the People, which did, and could only, make them lawful; but without Intention of drawing such a Practice into Precedent, or making it a standing Measure by which to proceed in all Times to come; and therefore we find their Counsels ever tended to keep Things as much as possible in the old Course. But soon after, an under Sett of Men, who had nothing to lose, and had neither born the Burthen nor Heat of the Day, found means to whisper in the King's Ear, that the Principles of Loyalty in the Church of *England*, were wholly inconsistent with the *Revolution*. Hence began the early Practice of caressing the Dissenters, reviling Universities, as Maintainers of Arbitrary Power, and reproaching the Clergy with the Doctrines of Divine-Right, Passive-Obedience, and Non-resistance. (*Examiner*, *PW* 3: 5–6; no. 13, 2 Nov. 1710)

Swift concedes that the enthronement of William III was a "[Breach] in the Succession," but one that was inevitable for national security reasons, which means that it was necessary to abandon the Catholic monarch, James II. Basically, politics must be kept "as much as possible in the old Course," and Swift refuses to make it an established "Precedent" to change the king artificially. As we have seen in chapter 2, section 2, he recognized that the abdication of James was and must be an extremely rare option to secure the maintenance of the ancient constitution in *The Sentiments of a Church-of-England Man*. Given this fact and the citation just above, it turns out that he has kept the recognition since even before he went under Harley's umbrella. An "under Sett of Men" indicates the Whigs, or more specifically the Junto, whom Swift satirically criticizes: they are blamed for undermining the stability of the Anglican establishment after the Revolution by means of religious toleration and the stigmatization of the clergy and church-goers as supporters of absolutism.

On the basis of this evaluation of the Revolution settlement, Swift assesses the contemporary state of the national constitution in *Examiner* no. 15:

> We live here under a limited Monarchy, and under the Doctrine and Discipline of an excellent Church: We are unhappily divided into two Parties, both which pretend a mighty Zeal for our Religion and Government, only they disagree about the Means. The Evils we must fence against are, on one side Fanaticism and Infidelity in Religion; and Anarchy, under the Name of a Commonwealth, in Government: On the other Side, Popery, Slavery, and the Pretender from *France*. (*PW* 3: 13)

When it comes to political system, a "limited Monarchy" here is virtually synonymous with a mixed monarchy, which consists of Crown, Lords, and Commons.[7] Royal authority is not absolute, but at the same time republicanism, labeled as "Anarchy, under the Name of a Commonwealth," is totally abhorred. Relatively, parliament seems to weigh in politics, but royal government should never be dissolved.[8] In the matter of religion, the Anglican establishment is supposed to be sustained firmly. On the one hand, Dissent is disdained for "Fanaticism and Infidelity," deserving to be excluded; on the other, adherence to Roman Catholicism is regarded as equivalent to "Slavery." Swift depicts the party division between Tory and Whig as an unhappy arrangement, but at the same time he admits that their differences lie in their "Means" rather than their ideas, according to which we may see that he does not count much on the fruits of power game among parties. For him, the politics of Britain can operate under the moderate constitutional monarchy; he is content with this current system, which is made up of an eclectic composition of Tory and Whig. We can notice that his basic political standpoint did not change, irrespectively of which party he backs. To put it more plainly, it is no exaggeration to say that his adherence to mixed monarchy — what is more, a thoroughly conservative type that attaches overriding importance to the Crown — could be one of his unshakable (though apparently elusive) beliefs behind his chameleonic political (or, more precisely, partisan) attitude.

In regard to the domestic administration, Swift castigates the corruption of the powers that be. He attributes the fall of the Godolphin ministry to the vices of the ministers concerned:

> [W]hoever thinks fit to revive that baffled Question, *Why was the late Ministry changed?* may receive the following Answer: That it was become necessary by the Insolence and Avarice of some about the QUEEN, who, in order to perpetuate their Tyranny, had made a monstrous Alliance with those who profess Principles destructive to our Religion and Government: [. . .] And indeed, the Ministry was changed for the same reason that Religion was reformed; because a thousand Corruptions had crept into the *Discipline* and *Doctrine* of the *State*, by the Pride, the Avarice, the Fraud, and the Ambition of those *who administered to us in Secular Affairs.* (*Examiner*, *PW* 3: 95; no. 29, 22 Feb. 1710–11)

Among others, the Duke of Marlborough becomes the main target of criticism. He is described as a grasping man in conspiracy with Godolphin for jobbery.[9] Yet Irvin Ehrenpreis points out:

> The faults for which he [Swift] mainly censures Marlborough are love of money and love of power, both of which appear amply allowed by careful historians. As for the number of Swift's published attacks, so far from being incessant over an extended period, they seem limited, before Marlborough's fall, to three *Examiners*[10] and *The Conduct of the Allies*, and afterwards to a poem, some brief mentions, and two or three longer references over two and a half

years. Later, Swift did bring out additional attacks or allusions, but none of these appeared during Marlborough's lifetime. (2: 526–27)

Despite launching severe (though apparently sporadic) reproaches against Marlborough, Swift recognizes his capacities. In *Journal to Stella*, he "gives his own view of Marlborough very honestly" (Davis, Introduction, Swift, *PW* 3: xvii):

> He [Marlborough] is covetous as Hell, and ambitious as the Prince of it: he would fain have been general for life, and has broken all endeavours for Peace, to keep his greatness and get money. [. . .] He fell in with all the abominable measures of the late ministry, because they gratified him for their own designs. Yet he has been a successful general, and I hope he will continue his command. (*Journal*, vol. 1, *PW* 15: 145; letter 12, 31 Dec. 1710)

Later, Swift casts doubt on the appropriateness of the Duke's removal from office before the conclusion of the peace treaty for the War of the Spanish Succession (1701–14) (Ehrenpreis 2: 532):

> [I]t is true that the duke of Marlborough is turned out of all [his employments]. [. . .] If the ministry be not sure of a Peace, I shall wonder at this step, and do not approve it at best. [. . .] I confess my belief, that he has not one good quality in the world besides that of a general, and even that I have heard denied by several great soldiers. But we have had constant success in arms while he commanded. Opinion is a mighty matter in war, and I doubt but the French think it impossible to conquer an army that he leads, and our soldiers think the same; and how far even this step may encourage the French to play tricks with us, no man knows. (*Journal*, vol. 2, *PW* 16: 452–53; letter 38, 1 Jan. 1711–12)

Swift does not mean to denounce the professional ability of the general. His attacks are directed primarily at "great man's greed" (Ehrenpreis 2: 533), which can result in the change of government. Turning now to his remarks on British diplomacy, Swift warns that corruption is encroaching inside and outside the country at a time: "[I]t will appear, by plain Matters of Fact, that no Nation was ever so long or so scandalously abused by the Folly, the Temerity, the Corruption, the Ambition of its domestick Enemies; or treated with so much Insolence, Injustice and Ingratitude by its foreign Friends" (*Conduct*, *PW* 6: 15). Moral decay is considered as the driving force of maladministration not only among the domestic factions but also among the European allies against France. He gives us a specific example in the *Conduct*:

> The War in *Spain* must be imputed to the Credulity of our Ministers, who suffered themselves to be persuaded by the Imperial Court, that the *Spaniards* were so violently affected to the House of *Austria* [. . .]. This we tried, and found the Emperor [Leopold I (1640–1705; r. 1658–1705)] to have deceived either Us or Himself: Yet there we drove on the War at a prodigious Disadvantage, with great Expence; And by a most corrupt Management, the only General, who by a Course of Conduct and Fortune almost miraculous, had nearly put us into Possession of the Kingdom, was left wholly unsupported, exposed to the Envy of his Rivals, disappointed by the Caprices of a young unexperienced Prince [Joseph I (1678–1711; r. 1705–1711)], under the Guidance of a rapacious *German* Ministry, and at last called home in Discontent: By which our Armies, both in *Spain* and *Portugal*, were made a Sacrifice to Avarice, Ill-conduct, or Treachery. (21)

Swift intends to claim that, whether at home or abroad, power-wielders possessed by degrading vices will almost inevitably fail to guide the ship of state. What is characteristic of his criticism is that as to both internal troubles and external threats, he puts more stress on condemnations directed against the character of the persons concerned, rather than on analyses of concrete events and policies. While he takes the offensive against the Whigs, meeting the demands of Harley's moderate scheme, he contends that political corruption arises from human depravity without regard to party or even to country.

In fact, frequently repeating the word in his tracts, Swift identifies avarice as the primary factor causing corruption in politics:

> There is no Vice which Mankind carries to such wild Extreams as that of *Avarice*: [. . .] [I]s Avarice perhaps the same Passion with Ambition, only placed in more ignoble and dastardly Minds; by which the Object is changed from *Power* to *Money?* Or, it may be, that one Man pursues Power in order to Wealth; and another Wealth, in order to Power; which last is the safer Way, although longer about; and, suiting with every Period, as well as Condition of Life, is more generally followed. (*Examiner*, *PW* 3: 80–81; no. 27, 8 Feb. 1710–11)

Avarice seeks after money or wealth, and ambition after power. When avarice combines with ambition, Swift claims, the worst effect will be brought about:

> Moralists make two kinds of Avarice; That of *Cataline* [Catiline (Lucius Sergius Catilina) (c. 108–62 BC)], *alieni appetens, sui profusus* ["covetous of another's possession, lavish of his own"]; and the other more generally understood by that Name; which is, the endless Desire of Hoarding: But I take the former to be more dangerous in a State, because it mingles well with Ambition, which I think the latter cannot; for, although the same Breast may capable

of admitting both, it is not able to cultivate them; and where the Love of heaping Wealth prevails, there is not, in my Opinion, much to be apprehended from Ambition. The Disgrace of that sordid Vice is sooner apt to spread than any other; and is always attended with the Hatred and Scorn of the People: So that whenever those two Passions happen to meet in the same Subject; it is not unlikely, that Providence hath placed *Avarice* to be a Check upon *Ambition* [. . .].

The Divine Authority of Holy Writ, the Precepts of Philosophers, the Lashes and Ridicule of Satyrical Poets, have been all employed in exploding this insatiable Thirst of Money [. . .]. (82)

The short quotation from Sallust (Gaius Sallustius Crispus) (c. 86–35/34 BC) heightens the impression that vice as exemplified by avarice and ambition is a universal abuse among political figures, as it is especially instrumental in practicing bribery. The multi-pronged attack, drawing from Scripture, philosophy, and popular lampoons, reflects the deep-seatedness of that "insatiable Thirst." In the *Conduct*, criticizing the errors of Godolphin and the Marlboroughs, Swift ventures to say that their covetousness encouraged Britain's commitment to the War of the Spanish Succession, yet he does not otherwise specify what was wrong with their policies:

[W]hen the Counsels of this War were debated in the late King's Time, my Lord *Godolphin* was then so averse from entring into it, that he rather chose to give up his Employment, and tell the King he could serve him no longer. Upon that Prince's Death, [. . .] this Lord thought fit to alter his Sentiments; for the Scene was quite changed; his Lordship, and the Family with whom he was engaged by so complicated an Alliance, were in the highest Credit possible with the Queen: The Treasurer's Staff was ready for his Lordship, the Duke was to Command the Army, and the Duchess [. . .] to be always nearest Her Majesty's Person; by which the whole Power, at Home and Abroad, would be devolved upon that Family. This was a Prospect so very inviting, that, to confess the Truth, it could not be easily withstood by any who have so keen an Appetite for Wealth or Ambition. [. . .] [W]hether this War were prudently begun or not, it is plain, that the true Spring or Motive of it, was the aggrandizing a particular Family, and in short, a War of the *General* and the *Ministry*, and not of the *Prince* or *People*; since those very Persons were against it when they knew the Power, and consequently the Profit, would be in other Hands. (*PW* 6: 40–41)

Swift asserts that "so keen an Appetite for Wealth or Ambition" was the principal cause of the involvement in the War, putting aside the validity of the political choice by the Godolphin administration — "whether this War were prudently begun or not." This pamphlet is targeted at Tory (or prospective Tory) supporters; its concentrated attack on the Whig participants serves to influence public and parliamentary opinion toward peace. We should notice, however, that Swift chooses to portray avarice as having the irresistible capacity to *proselytize* these major figures; he does not portray their characters as originally bad. Earlier in the *Examiner*, he mentions:

The wisest Prince on Earth may be forced, by the Necessity of his Affairs, and the present Power of an unruly Faction, or deceived by the Craft of ill designing Men: One or two Ministers, most in his Confidence, may *at first* have good Intentions, but grow corrupted by Time, by Avarice, by Love, by Ambition, and have fairer Terms offered them, to gratify their Passions or Interests, from *one Set of Men* than another, until they are too far involved for a Retreat; and so be forced to take *seven Spirits more wicked than themselves.* (*PW* 3: 16; no. 15)

Avarice can easily undermine one's principles: it even changes "good Intentions" into a "*wicked*" spirit. Swift, who tends to "put principle above party" (Lock, *Swift's Tory Politics* 136), consistently emphasizes that those who allow greed to impair their integrity rank as the most treacherous representatives of political order.

As he assigns greater value to morality and philosophy than to policies, it is almost obvious that Swift takes little account of party politics. To delve into the idiosyncrasy of Swift's bipartisan manner, we shall shift our attention to Harley's "non-party designs" or "moderate anti-party feelings" (Downie, *Robert Harley* 72, 118), clandestinely but vividly described in *Plaine English to All Who Are Honest, or Would Be So If They Knew How,* and examine the extent to which they affected Swift's commissioned propaganda activities.

4. The Political Ideals of "Robin the Trickster"

Plaine English is a manuscript tract that "was never published in Harley's lifetime" (Downie, *Robert Harley* 106), but reveals his "private" political views (Speck and Downie 101), in spite of the difficulty in grasping his real intention due to his famous "devious and indirect" disposition (100). It was targeted at country gentlemen with the aim of reproaching Godolphin and Marlborough, who took the reins of government in the early and middle years of the reign of Queen Anne (1665–1714; r. 1702–14). Harley, who was originally a radical Whig but converted to a Tory, had teamed up with them as the Speaker of the Commons, but he later came into collision with them, as Godolphin placed greater reliance on the Whigs, affiliated with the moneyed interest, so that his ministry could expect a better handling of the government and continue the War of the Spanish Succession "at the expense of the country gentlemen" (Downie, *Robert Harley* 74). Harley himself was a typical country gentleman (Matsuzono 175), and he "wanted to end the war at the earliest available opportunity" so as to conclude a peace and reduce the financial burden of the landed interest (Downie, *Robert Harley* 74). At the time of writing *Plaine English*, Harley was defeated in the power game against the duumvirate, and he temporarily went into opposition. Then "Robin the Trickster" began to make arrangements for overthrowing the Godolphin ministry and attempted to demonstrate the logic for criticizing its mischief. However, under the cloak of its attacks on the abuse of power and the pursuit of private profit by the Court, *Plaine English* discloses Harley's own political ideals, which are generally considered as not easily visible because of his reservedness (Harley 100–01; Matsuzono 171–89). To encourage the unity of the nation in the teeth of both domestic and foreign pressures, Harley represents before us a common ground — by showing a firm adherence to the ancient constitution — that would be agreeable to a conservative climate of the country instead of a Tory-Whig party labeling.

One of the most conspicuous characteristics of Harley's political thought displayed in *Plaine English* is that he emphasizes the risk of party politics. In the midst of his criticism of the duumvirs, Harley claims:

Their chiefest Art is to keep up Factions amongst us. This they learnt in that *virtuous Court* where they had their education, but they have far out done those times. The nation was then divided into those who were jealous for their Liberty & Property on the one hand, & others who were alarmd with the fear of a designe to overthrow the church & monarchy. And tho now the foundations of those Partys are abolished; yet is the Fury & Rage stil kept up by wicked arts: let me Appeal to you al both whigs and torys from what quarter you have reason to fear Danger, do but confer notes together, & you wil find the same Persons have every year amused Each of you, & raild at one Party to the other, while they cheated and abused you both. Nay there is not that single person who they draw in to meet them but they have either ungratefully requited themselves deserted, or Basely deceivd, and wil you still go on blinded with mutual Rage agst each other while they warme themselves at your intestine fires & are secured by your wilful blindness. O fellow citizens no longer let this reproach ly upon you [. . .]. (106)

He offers a cutting remark on the Court interest, cynically calling it "that *virtuous Court*." He regards party split as the quintessence of "wicked" maneuvers by the powers that be, most supposedly the Whig Junto. The so-called rage of party is made and maintained by "the same Persons" who deceive and exploit both Tories and Whigs, and it will finally lead all those to "wilful blindness" to the truth of politics. The Court manipulates information among the factions by "[railing] at one Party to the other" and vice versa, and stirs up their internal feud endlessly in order to secure its profits.

Accordingly, Harley makes an "Appeal" to both parties for opening their eyes (he compares his audience to Samson and encourages them to have his "courage" and "strength") and joining hands with each other regardless of their ideological differences to preserve "the Public weal" against the "common enemy" (106–07):

Unite upon common Principles, agst those who rend you & then you wil quickly give the enemies to the Public *their just Doom*. Consider this & be no longer tools to those who make a prey of you & recommend themselves to each Party by slandering the other. Let me ask you seriously have you any regard to ye Principles

90

each of you profess? Then how can you *promote* the interest of
those who study to overturne everything either of you would set
up, & have no pretence to any Principle but to dash you to peices
agst one another, in order to set up themselves. (107)

The "enemies" almost certainly indicate the Marlboroughs and
Godolphin. Harley's aversion to party politics seems to be inflamed
by the duumvirs' abuse of power and wealth. Marlborough was the
Captain General and Godolphin the Lord Treasurer at the time, and
they were able to control patronage to strengthen their political and
financial foundation. Harley points out that the excessive dominance
of the Court in general, and of the duumvirate in particular, induces
"flattery," "mean submissions," and "an unlimited obedience to all their
commands." He sharply blames them for the dissipation of the "Public
Purse" for "private use" to "enrich" the "overgrown" Marlborough
family and shows evident disgust at the "uninhabitable" Blenheim
Palace, that is, Queen Anne's tremendous reward for the victory in
the Battle of Blenheim in the War of the Spanish Succession, which
had placed enormous burden on the national finance. On the whole,
Harley detests the monopoly of the Court for office and war profit as
Godolphin and Marlborough take a tight grip on them. For him, it looks
as if their factional dynamics are undermining the power and function
of parliament (104–06).[11]

It is noticeable that Harley expresses his hatred for the Court
favorites by way of using the rhetoric of avarice repeatedly. To take an
example, he writes:

And thus my Honest Countrymen, I have given you a very short
view of great mischiefs, those you feel, those wch you at present
groan under, & such until God be merciful and the Parliamt
virtuous & boldly exert themselves, you & yr posterity wil for ever

be subjected to through an insatiable avarice & boundless thirst of Power [. . .]. (106)

Avarice is an inveterate disease which will torment not only the country "at present" but also its "posterity" forever. Harley tries to insist that the powers that be are apt to be obsessed by "an insatiable avarice & boundless thirst," which could breed corruption — "Bountiful corrupters of other mens Truth" (105) — in the political world. In other words, corruption in politics, triggered by avarice, will taint those in power and change them into "those who rend you" into factions (107). He would like to suggest that the party struggle will hide the truth from those in parliament (particularly the Country) and cause political chaos, from which only the favorites can reap profits, and that will derail the "necessary services of ye nation" (105). Hence he seeks to pursue the common good and, for that very purpose, requests the Tories and the Whigs to "[u]nite upon common Principles" beyond party limitations (107):

> Be no longer drawn to be their sport by y^r quarrels but act together upon these Principles for the Public good in wch you agree: be not deceived, even they may pretend they have some Principles, but center al in themselves. Profit & power are what they only adore & can never be satisfied with *either*. See their picture exactly drawne. The Horse Leach hath two daughters, Crying give give. There are three that are never satisfied, yea, four say not, it is enough. (109)

Harley stresses that men of both sides should not fall prey to the artifice of particular men in authority anymore. It seems quite reasonable, therefore, that his fundamental political ideal aims to avoid party division and confront in a body the desire of the Court for "Profit & power" — each deplored in Swift's pamphlets as the prey of avarice and

92

ambition producing corruption — in order to realize the "Public good."

Let us now shift our focus to revealing the "common Principles" which Harley possesses (107). As to the national polity, he is clearly in favor of the ancient constitution. Presumably as a converted Tory, he gives a positive assessment of the Tory principles: "The principle you profess is to secure monarchy & the church, to Preserve the Constitution in Crowne L^{ds} & Commons" (107–08). His inclination toward the mixed government is also expressed in the early part of *Plaine English* recollecting the Restoration period. He states as follows:

> [T]he King [Charles II] & his ministers began to betake themselves to Business, & to forme themselves upon some model. The nobility, the gentry, & the clergy, were faithful & loyal. but alas. If the courtiers joynd with these it must be upon a true foundation. For tho' during the *Love fit* at the Restauration they had made great concessions; yet as soon as the Honymoon was over, the old Cavaliers, & Parliamenteers joynd to Preserve the Liberty of the Country: This was a mortal Crime. these as now *our* ministers having other designs, must find other tools. They could not trust themselves in such hands; therefore Partys must be made & kept up in the nation: for they act by this Principle, to divide the nation into Partys, then to joyne with that wch is the most unreasonable, that they in returne may be more devoted to them, & more ready to assist them *in all* their *avaritious* & ambitious Practices. (103)

Harley presents the combination of Lords ("the clergy" and "the nobility") and Commons ("the gentry") under monarchic rule as a certain type of political "model." The model would have realized on a "true foundation" if the "courtiers" had cooperated in its formation. He again criticizes the Court, whose lack of commitment to the harmony of political power restored the division between Royalists and

Parliamentarians, later transforming into the conflict between Tories and Whigs. In his view both sides went hand in hand to maintain the "Liberty" (almost nearly the licentiousness) of national politics. It is after all obvious that he condemns party strife, which would "divide the nation" and undermine the stability of the constitution. He describes the discord persistently supported by avarice as "a mortal Crime." Interestingly enough, in the passage where he refers to the old Whig principles, Harley also shows some understanding of them:

> Consider o ye whiggs what it was gave you Credit & Reputation, upon what Principles you divided & distinguished yr selves from others. In former days were you not agst favourites standing between the crown & the People? [. . .] [W]ere you not agst setting up officers & furnishing them with mony to oppose Country Gentlemen? (107)

As he was once a radical Whig, it seems that he had felt a certain sympathy for some progressive policies as well as for Country Toryism. His focus of criticism is consistently on the Court interest predominating the workings of parliament. All the more because he does not dwell on the Tory-Whig party differences in this manner, he sticks to the "common Principles" serviceable to the nation at large, and the advocacy of the mixed and balanced constitution is an eminently suitable instrument for persuading various factions generally in the midst of conservatization.

Another key component is that Harley champions the Protestant succession:

> Having thus spoken plainly to my countrymen as they are divided under the two Parties as yet kept up by dark Arts. Some things there are in wch the Honest men of al Parties agree. I mean the Preferring her Present ma^{tie} & securing the Protestant Succes-

sion, according to ye laws & our repeated oths to such let me observe how lately we have been threatend with an invasion. Could this have been attempted without enemys? It is then y^r Duty O my Countrymen! to examine whence this arose, tho these close practices may not perhaps, without some [   ] be detected, yet the Dark Lanthorne wil give light enough to every considering honest Britain to show him who is ye Guido Faux who carryes it. (108; brackets in the text)

He argues that "Honest men of al Parties" should support Protestant monarchs whose succession is regulated by law, rather than by blood. Here he deliberately expresses his approval of the Act of Settlement (1701), which secured the succession to the House of Hanover to exclude the Stuart Catholic Pretender, James Francis Edward Stuart (1688–1766). Harley's fear of "invasion" undoubtedly comes from France, and the culprit is likened to "Guido Faux" [Guy Fawkes] (1570–1606), the notorious Catholic ringleader in the Gunpowder Plot (1605). To such an extent Harley despises Francophilia and popery as a threat to the safety of the British constitution.

What is more, Harley warns at the end of *Plaine English* as below:

Consider what y^r Duty to ye crowne requires of you. Consider what y^r country & y^r posterity require of you, & be assurd that as soon as they see you have purgd out ye opium you have taken, & begin to rouse y^r selves & act upon true principles, these Heathen magicians wil never stand before you. (109)

National crises, whether domestic or foreign, are depicted as "opium" which must be cleaned up, and enemies to Britain are compared to "Heathen magicians." Considering the context of his argument, the intensification of party conflict and the influence of Catholics and

France would be his chief apprehensions regarding internal troubles
and external threats, respectively. In order to surmount these problems
at home and abroad, Harley proposes to men of both parties a moderate
political regime which sets the security and the solidarity of (Anglican)
church and state as its mainstay. It is no wonder that his principles are
constructed by an ideological hybrid between, or rather, beyond the
dual party lines, for they mirror his resolute preference of national
interests to party ones in the face of the perils to the nation.

Harley is well-known for his frequent changes of sides — from a
radical Whig to a Country statesman to a Court politician to an Opposition member and finally to the first minister of the Tory government.
That is definitely one of the main reasons why he was called Robin
the Trickster, but he was not a mere political chameleon. His basic
philosophy is consistent in advocating the Country ideas and in
rallying support for country gentlemen, with a disposition to slough off
the dependence on the two-party system (Matsuzono 188). "After the
removal of Godolphin," as J. A. Downie points out, Harley "showed a
willingness to live happily with the remnant of the old government."
What he wanted is "to *abolish* the distinction between the parties, not
exchange one set of party men for another" (*Robert Harley* 118). It
can safely be said that his apparently opportunistic attitude embodies
his moderate scheme to avert the disunion between Toryism and
Whiggism, and at heart he hopes to maintain the ancient constitution
which mediates between absolute monarchy and excessive democracy.
Moreover, his thought is certainly consonant with the English conservative tradition: it upholds the limited monarchy which ideally sets the
Protestant sovereign to prevent the erosion of Roman Catholicism.

5. Between Allegiance and Independence: Swift's Idiosyncratic Affinity with Harley's Political Designs

Harley's political ideals show great similarities to the seemingly opportunistic conservatism of the Marquess of Halifax, who praised the English mixed constitution as the best "Composite" in which "dominion and Liberty are so happyly reconciled" (*Character* 194). He also expressed his animosity against France — calling it "a forreign Trespasser" (237) — and his wariness of papism. Although Harley did not give any direct reference to Halifax in *Plaine English*, the former was actually "on very intimate terms with Halifax from 1693," two years before the death of the latter (Downie, *Robert Harley* 27). The Trickster, who was originally a radical "Shaftesburian whig of the old school" but later opposed the Whig Junto (19), must have been fairly conversant with the past performance of the Trimmer, who was engaged in a hot discussion on the Exclusion Bill with the Earl of Shaftesbury, an eminent leader of the Whigs at the time. Added to this, allowing for the history of the theory of the ancient constitution in the early modern period, which we traced in chapter 1, Harley's thought partakes of a certain level of ideological universality, and it should be fair to say that he is eligible to add his name to the list of English conservative thinkers.

Furthermore, the general tone of Harley's argument is strongly projected onto the "Tory" tracts by Swift. In the *Examiner* and the *Conduct*, we can see a close resemblance in the trimmer-like stance, the criticism of party politics, the concept of the national polity, and the aversion to avarice. It is obviously true that Swift sufficiently fulfilled his role to carry out the mission from Harley as a Tory propagandist. In reality, his pamphlets made a substantial contribution to inducing public and parliamentary opinion to advocate the peace for the War of the Spanish Succession. However, we can also find Swift's elaborate individuality behind his ostensible loyalty to Harley's strategy. For example, looking back to section 3, in terms of the perception about the present state of affairs, Swift boldly reprobated Dissenting worship as one of the rejectable "Evils" in religion, despite Harley being of Presbyterian origin.[12] Swift's advocacy of mixed monarchy in conjunction with his antipathy to republicanism and his hatred of Catholic despotism remained unchanged since he was still in the Whig camp and wrote the *Discourse*, that is, before he became acquainted with Harley (*Examiner*, *PW* 3: 13; no. 15). The revulsion against the insatiable desire of the Godolphin administration for wealth and power was shared between the two, but, unlike Harley, who actively worked on Marlborough's dismissal from office, Swift appreciated the Captain's ability. Meanwhile, it should not also be forgotten that another ally of Swift, Henry St John, Viscount Bolingbroke, who was a high Tory, argued against the Whigs concerning the War in *A Letter to the Examiner* (writ. 1710, pub. 1712) to push an uncompromising scheme for more relentless pursuit of their misconduct: "The Members of the *Bank*, the *Dutch*, and the Court of *Vienna*, are call'd in as Confederates to the [Godolphin] *Ministry*, and such an Indignity is offer'd to the Crown, as no Man, who has the Honour of his Country at Heart, can with Patience hear" (226). For more details, Bolingbroke later writes in *Letters on the Study and Use of History* (writ. 1735–36) in retrospect:

[T]hey [Whigs] not only continued to abet the emperor, [. . .] but the Dutch likewise [. . .]. Upon such schemes [. . .] was the opposition to the treaty of Utrecht carried on: and the means employed, and the means projected to be employed, were worthy of such schemes; open, direct, and indecent defiance of legal authority, secret conspiracies against the state, and base machinations against particular men, who had no other crime than that of endeavouring to conclude a war, under the authority of the queen, which a party in the nation endeavoured to prolong, against her authority. (*Boling-broke's Defence* 125–26; letter 8)

In order to heighten criticism of the Whigs, Swift adopted this conspiracy thesis. It invited Harley's vigilance against radicality, insomuch as Swift was removed from the editorship of the *Examiner*, though Harley later sought reconciliation to make him write the *Conduct* (Downie, *Robert Harley* 134–38). The fact can reveal that Swift was not merely under the parallel influence of Bolingbroke; rather, Swift attempted to embrace the ideas and principles by which he can grasp the direction of his argument at his own will. Actually, Swift in turn showed a delicate reluctance to unconditionally extol the "*Tory Principle*" in the *Conduct* (*PW* 6: 42), as we have seen in section 2. It is likely that his scrupulous display of pride as an Anglican clergyman and an ambitious writer with an independent mind did not allow him to necessarily remain within the purview of Harley's vision.

In sum, while he performed his duty as a Tory pamphleteer, Swift subtly infiltrated his own views into the works commissioned by the chief minister. Although he certainly blackened the character of the Whigs, he did not cling to the differentiation of party itself, and rather betrayed his dissatisfaction of factionalism. His sense of danger centered on tracing the root of political corruption to the degeneration of human morals underlying the defects in Tory-Whig political measures or principles. The tenor of Swift's conservative rhetoric to put forward an ideal image of the state was consistent before and after his party conversion. As he did not come under pressure to "markedly alter his political opinions on entering Harley's camp" (Downie, *Robert Harley* 128), it was Swift who chose to avail himself of Harley's timely offer and his cause. In other words, Swift was not exactly partial to the Tories, but seems to have pinned his hopes for correcting the nation on the moderate Harley administration which belonged to the governing party at that time. In a manner similar to that of the two parties that explored their different "Means" to realize their apparently same political and religious purpose in an effort to preserve the security of the country, as he describes in the *Examiner* (*PW* 3: 13; no. 15), Swift made the fullest possible use of the guise of a Tory spokesman as the "Means" to disseminate the ideas that had been rooted in the English conservative tradition in order to defend the national polity from the dangers both at home and abroad.

Chapter 4

Swift's Politics as a Would-Be Historiographer
His Unpublished Works at the Change of Dynasty
and *Gulliver's Travels*

1. The Political and Ideological Significance of Swift's Unpublished Papers

While the negotiations for the Treaty of Utrecht (1713) were proceeding, the dissension between Robert Harley and Henry St John was growing more intense. This internal strife behind the tactical progress in English diplomacy was about to bring on the twilight of the Tory administration. Around that time, driven by a sense of responsibility to leave a right record of the achievements of Queen Anne and the Harley ministry to posterity, Swift wrote *The History of the Four Last Years of the Queen* (writ. 1712–13, pub. 1758). However, since its subjective and candid tone was regarded as likely to provoke the Opposition and to be prejudicial to the government line in favor of the peace negotiations to end the War of the Spanish Succession, he could not win the cooperation of both Oxford and Bolingbroke in publishing the *History*. Later, even after the overthrow of the Harley ministry, Swift planned its publication more than once. In 1736, he had a design for inserting into it, or combining with it, *Memoirs, Relating to That Change Which Happened in the Queen's Ministry in the Year 1710* and *An Enquiry into the Behaviour of the Queen's Last Ministry, with Relation to Their Quarrells among Themselves, and the Design Charged upon Them of Altering the Succession of the Crown* (writ. 1715–c. 1720, pub. 1765) (Davis and Eherenpreis xxxvii). In fact, *Memoirs* and the *Enquiry* were "companion pieces" to the *History* (Williams: xii):[1] the

[100]

three works do have a homogeneous character, as expressions of his own views on politics in the form of historical writing. Also in *Some Free Thoughts upon the Present State of Affairs* (writ. 1714, pub. 1741), Swift gave a "cool analysis" of the political situation which "provides in part a defence, in part a criticism of the Treasurer" (Davis and Eherenpreis xxv). It should be noted that he did not find any necessity to alter its contents for more than twenty years after Anne's death (xxvii), as in the case of the *Enquiry* (xxxviii).

Most of these writings were projected in the unsettled period in which the change of dynasty and government took place, but were kept unpublished against his wishes while he was alive and well. They were not intended for a general readership; they did not seek to influence public opinion. "[A]t the close of his public life in London," as Herbert Davis and Irvin Ehrenpreis point out, Swift "gives his views on politics and politicians, writing in the mood of one who has already withdrawn from the centre of action, and was keeping himself aloof even before he went into the country" (xxv). Of the *History*, Ehrenpreis remarks: "It contains a number of passages revealing Swift's peculiar views on topics close to him, sometimes contradicting or even censuring the judgment of his ministerial friends" (2: 604).[2] He also maintains that in *Some Free Thoughts* Swift obviously expresses his own policies (739–40). These inconspicuous works can thus reveal Swift's consistent political beliefs, enunciated from a standpoint that is more detached from the Tory-Whig tug of war than were his previous Tory-commissioned pamphlets such as *The Examiner* and *The Conduct of the Allies*.

Scholars, irrespective of the difference between their Tory and Whig interpretations of Swift, can agree in recognizing that he held coherent principles beyond party allegiance. For example, W. A. Speck argues: "[A]lthough [. . .] inconsistency might be expected of a man who changed from Whig to Tory between 1704 and 1714, Swift's transference of his allegiance cannot be attributed to a change of principles" ("From Principles to Practice" 80). Notwithstanding that Swift drew a clearer distinction between Tory and Whig when he dealt with the "concrete question of peace or war," he "never sacrificed consistency with regard to Church and State, and so never fully appreciated the real division between the English parties on these abstract issues" (83). Hence, in order to deepen the discussion on his political thought, it is critically significant to wake up to the importance of his *uncommissioned* papers, which were written in the latter part of his palmy years, as well as his Tory tracts on behalf of the Harley ministry, for he wrote them with an autonomous spirit, identifying himself as the right person to be a historiographer, not as a hired partisan author.

2. Swift's Unchanging Political Creed

The basic principles of Swift's political outlook are, in a sense, more clearly exposed in his writings of this period. First of all, Swift again shows his loyalty to Anglicanism. In *Some Free Thoughts*, he writes:

> There are two Points of the highest Importance, wherein a very great Majority of the Kingdom appear perfectly hearty and unanimous. First, that the Church of England should be preserved entire in all Her [Anne's] Rights, Powers and Priviledges; All Doctrines relating to Government discouraged which She condemns; All Schisms, Sects and Heresies discountenanced and kept under due Subjection, as far as consists with the Lenity of our Constitution. Her open Enemies (among whom I include at least Dissenters of all Denominations) not trusted with the smallest Degree of Civil or Military Power; and Her secret Adversaries under the Names of Whigs, Low-Church, Republicans, Moderation-Men, and the like,

receive no Marks of Favour from the Crown, but what they should deserve by a sincere Reformation. (*PW* 8: 88)

The clergyman of the Church of Ireland with enthusiastic aspirations for a high position in England firmly upholds the stability of the Anglican establishment, especially the dominance of the High Church. The assumed close tie between church and state is openly emphasized, and his animus against other sects looks more plainly released than in his previous writings. As a proof of this, Swift intentionally jumbles up political and religious enemies to the nation: any type of dissent — by "Whigs, Low-Church, Republicans, Moderation-Men, and the like" — must be excluded from secular and royal decision-making machinery. In the *History*, his bitter hostility to such "Dissenters of all Denominations" is specifically seen in his criticism of foreign Protestants, Scottish Presbyterians, and Quakers (*PW* 7: 94, 96, 106). They are all censured as intractable obstacles to Anglican worship, as it is quite difficult for them to adapt themselves to the established system of governance in Britain.[3] In Swift's mind, there can be no compromise on the basis for forming an ideal society, namely, the recognition of the Established Church as the foundation of the nation, and that may be why he chooses to take a more severe attitude to toleration than ever before, standing on the verge of the overthrow of the Tory ministry which can put the brakes on a Dissenting trend.

Secondly, Swift repeatedly defends securing the Protestant succession by transferring the royal house to Hanover. Following the first point as cited above, he declares in *Some Free Thoughts*:

The other Point of great Importance is the Security of the Protestant Succession in the House of Hannover; not from any Partiality to that Illustrious House, further than as it hath had the Honour to mingle with the Blood Royal of England, and is the nearest Branch of our Regal Line reformed from Popery. (*PW* 8: 90)

Then he totally rejects Roman Catholicism and severely criticizes the Old Pretender, James Francis Edward Stuart:

> [I]t may very impartially be pronounced, that the Number of those who wish to see the Son of the abdicated Prince upon the Throne, is altogether inconsiderable. And further, I believe it will be found, that there are None who so much dread any Attempt he shall make for the Recovery of his imagined Rights, as the Roman-Catholicks of England, who love their Freedom and Properties too well, to desire his Entrance by a French Army, and a Field of Blood [. . .].
>
> As to the Person of this nominall Prince, he lyes under all manner of Disadvantages: The Vulgar imagin him to have been a Child imposed upon the Nation by the fraudulent Zeal of his Parents and their bigotted Councellors; [. . .] and, a counterfeit Conversion will be too gross to pass upon the Kingdom after what we have seen and suffered from the like Practice in his Father. He is likewise said to be of weak Intellectualls, and an unsound Constitution. [. . .] He is utterly unknown in England, which he left in the Cradle [. . .]. (91)

Thus Swift presses the illegitimacy of the Pretender, in parallel with treating his father, James II, as an "abdicated Prince," not as one deposed by the people, which means that Swift is continuously unwilling to acknowledge the Glorious Revolution as a civil one. In fact, he insists that the reason for supporting the legitimacy of the Revolution settlement and of the accession of William III, even among "the highest Tories," is to maintain "the present Establishment" both "in Church and State" and justify the Protestant succession in the House of Hanover (92). Furthermore, he advocates that the grandson of George I (1660–1727; r. 1714–27), Frederick Louis (1707–51), be brought to England in his early childhood so that he can be educated in the English style suited to a British monarch, after the example of William, who "was no Stranger to our Language or Manners, and went often to the Chappel of His Princess" (93, 95–96). Even after the start of the Hanoverian dynasty, Swift writes in the *Enquiry* with a touch of regret:

> For my own Part, I freely told my Opinion to the Ministers; and did afterwards offer many Reasons for it in a Discourse intended for the Publick, (but stopped by the Queen's Death) that the young Grandson (whose Name I cannot remember) should be invited over to be educated in England; by which I conceived, the Queen might be secure from the Influence of Cabals and Factions, the Zealots who affected to believe the Succession in Danger could have no Pretences to complain, and the Nation might one day hope to be governed by a Prince of English Manners and Language, as well as acquainted with the true Constitution of Church and State; And this was the Judgment of those at the Helm before I offered it; neither were they or their Mistress to be blamed that such a Resolution was not pursued: perhaps from what hath since happened, the Reader will be able to satisfy himself. (*PW* 8: 179; ch. 2)

Clearly Swift noticed that George was disposed toward the Whigs (especially the Court Whigs, described as "Cabals and Factions") rather than toward Anne and the Harley ministry. He inclines to sarcastic remarks about George, who was poor at speaking English and cared little about adapting himself to English manners. However, Swift's concern with the continuation of the Protestant line prevails over his misgivings. Even if he disliked the king as an individual, he could not favor Jacobites or Dissenters, so he adhered to the choice which would maintain the Anglican Church regime.

Thirdly, Swift continues to uphold the concept of the ancient constitution. As we have seen in *A Discourse of the Contests and Dissensions in Athens and Rome*, written when he took sides with the Whigs, and in the *Examiner*, written when he worked as a Tory propagandist, Swift accepts the mixed monarchy of Crown, Lords, and Commons. Further in the *History*, he argues:

He [Harley] considered the House of Peers as a Body made up almost a Fourth Part of New Men within Twenty Years past; all Clients or Proselytes to the Leaders of the opposite Party, and consequently stocked with Principles little consistent with the old Constitution: [. . .] That, where the Two Houses should differ so far as to stop the Course of Business, the Commons must of necessity comply, or be dissolved; which would put the Prince and People under insuperable Difficulties, and make it ruinous, or impossible for a Ministry to serve: That, the Royal Prerogative could never be more properly exerted than in such an Exigency as this [. . .]. (*PW* 7: 19–20)

[I]n such a Government as this, where the Prince holds the Balance between Two great Powers, the Nobility and People; It is of the very nature of his Office to remove from One Scale into Another; or sometimes put his own Weight into the lightest, so to bring both to an Equilibrium: And [. . .] the other Party had been above Twenty Years corrupting the Nobility with Republican Principles, which nothing but the Royal Prerogative could hinder from overspreading us. (20–21)

While criticizing the Whigs for spreading "Republican Principles," which are "little consistent with the old Constitution," Swift reveals his ideal of how parliamentary politics should be managed, partly on the pretense of introducing the political thinking of Harley. The Lords and the Commons are considered as the "Two great Powers," but he accepts that it is the Commons which must "comply" when the two Houses cannot reach an agreement, in which case the royal prerogative is best employed.[4] He expects the Crown to work as an arbiter between the Lords and the Commons, not as an absolute monarch. What is most important here is that Swift continues to adopt the image of scales to describe the function of mixed government as in the *Discourse*, as previously noted in chapter 1, section 1. Although he appears to be still in deference to the Tories at this point, he consistently uses the same metaphor as when he made his debut in the republic of letters as a Whig advocate, in order to expound the theory of mixed monarchy.

In the long run, it turns out that Swift tenaciously attempted to weave into his political discourses, whether Whig, Tory, or possibly independent, his conservative ideas of what the state should be, behind his trimming attitude to interparty dynamics. This can lead us to realize his constant pride and efforts to secure political independence, and also the unyielding potential of the concept of the mixed constitution, in the midst of the rage of party. Now in order to explain Swift's political standpoint more elaborately, it may be quite effective to peruse *Memoirs*, particularly by contrast with Daniel Defoe and one of his minor but important tracts, *The Secret History of the White-Staff*.[5]

3. Swift versus Defoe: A "Secret History" of Swift's *Memoirs*

Defoe and Swift are famous for acting as chief propagandists in the employment of Harley. During his regime in the reign of Queen Anne, Harley made much account of their power of the pen to manipulate public opinion, but the two talented writers are also known for making very little mention of each other in their writings, in spite of sharing a fierce sense of rivalry between them. Although numerous studies have been made to clarify the nature of their political and literary relations, there is still much difficulty in specifying which of one's works exactly had a direct effect on which of the other's.[6] With this background in mind, it is worth pointing out that Davis and Ehrenpreis give us a precious hint for their rare point of contact. They suggest that Swift's *Memoirs* (writ. Oct. 1714) may have been "prompted" by the appearance of Defoe's *Secret History* (pub. c. Sept. 1714). The latter is suspected to have used "material supplied by Oxford" (xxx). Harley tried to deny the rumor that he gave a hand to its publication, but Defoe is presumed to have been in consultation with him to write it (Downie, *Robert Harley* 187–88; Shiotani, *Daniel Defoe* 253–54).[7] Taking Swift's jealous and competitive temper into account, it is little wonder that Swift gave an immediate reaction to Defoe's project.

From the outset, both tracts were the fruits of their attempts to defend the previous Harley ministry after the death of the queen. Former Tory leaders Harley and St John were about to be impeached at the start of the reign of George I and the accompanying Whig supremacy. By publishing the *Secret History*, Defoe vindicated the conduct of Harley in office, even though this "Robin the Trickster," notorious for his opportunism, broke off his connections with Defoe and the press on this occasion.[8] On the other hand, Swift's *Memoirs* was not published in his lifetime. He had to flee to Ireland as Harley was ousted from power. Swift hoped that *Memoirs* would serve as "an entertainment to those who will have any personal regard for me or my memory" (*PW* 8: 107), but he can be thought to plead against the criticism toward Harley (Davis and Ehrenpreis xxx; Downie, *Jonathan Swift* 204). According to J. A. Downie, Swift felt as if he were in "exile" in his homeland, and his sense of isolation after the fall of the Tory administration caused him to "[justify] his own conduct, and the actions of his friends" (*Jonathan Swift* 203, 204).

The common point is that, at this delicate time (the change of dynasty from Stuart to Hanover and that of government from Tory to Whig), both Defoe and Swift, on the decline of their presence within political circles, exerted themselves to champion the character and conduct of their quondam patron, which would lead them to stand their ground as ministerial pamphleteers. This literary synchronicity, which seems very unlikely to be coincidental, can entice us to make a comparative examination of the *Secret History* and *Memoirs*. The focus will be put on how and in what respect Swift set up against Defoe's discourse. Although they are generally considered minor tracts, this will open a fresh vista to the reading of their works and their literary activities.

Defoe's *Secret History* is not a "history" in the literal sense. It contains an abundance of fictional inventions: in particular the scene of Harley's resignation of the Lord Treasurer can be regarded as "the best example of his fictional skill" (Downie, Explanatory Notes 397). On that account, though we need to take Defoe's voice with a pinch of salt, we may say that the *Secret History* shows his willingness to defend Harley all the more elaborately.

The beginning part of the *Secret History* is constituted by the criticism against the mismanagement of the ministry of Sidney Godolphin. This is a typical way of justifying Harley's grip on power at the time. What seems to be characteristic in Defoe's statement is that he blames the Godolphin ministry for the failure to deal with the impeachment of Henry Sacheverell (1674?–1724), who inflamed pro-Anglican sentiment among the masses and triggered the collapse of the Whig Junto administration. Defoe, a well-known Presbyterian, understandably calls this High-Church clergyman "that worthless [Man]," but at the same time he criticizes the ministry's unskillful handling of the case. In his eyes, in the process of disposing of Sacheverell, the ministry lapsed into "acting as it were against the Church Interest it self, which they all were Members of," so that it "gave another Party [the Tories] room to break in upon them, and at once both to supplant their Power, and their Persons" (*Secret History* 266). Added to this, Defoe picks up Harley's dismissal from the Secretary of State for the Northern Department in 1708 (the year when Harley wrote *Plaine English*) as "concurring Mistakes" of the ministry:

> [T]hey knew that they were not able to supplant him [Harley] in the Favour of the Queen, or prevent Her Majesty giving him distinguishing Marks of Favour, even before their Faces, and also taking her Measures from his Councils, in Contradiction to the Steps which they had often taken, and which sometimes gave them the Mortification of silently squaring their Measures by his Schemes [. . .].
>
> This secret Fire they neglected at first, and impolitickly suffer'd so long to encrease, till it broke out into a Flame, which they could never quench; and continuing obstinately to oppose the restoring that one Minister, [. . .] they lost the Queen herself, and by Consequence fell from the Administration, and were supplanted by that Hand, which they had not thought worth their while to apprehend any Danger from. (267)

Defoe maintains that, since Godolphin underestimated Harley's ability and credibility, he and the Whigs lost the reins of government and the aegis of the queen. Through this rhetoric, Defoe glamorizes the legitimacy and effectiveness of the advent of the Harley ministry.

The major part of the *Secret History* consists of the reproach to St John and his confederates as they threatened Harley's handling of government from inside the Tory party. For one thing, Defoe calls the October Club "a set of High, Hot, out of Temper Politicians, whose view was within themselves, and who acting upon Principles of absolute Government, pushed at establishing their Party in a Power or Capacity of Governing by the Severity of the Law" (*Secret History* 273). As St John was famous for his radical conservativeness and had a regular conflict with Harley, who pursued middle-of-the-road policies, the members of the Club would look forward to the former seizing the political initiative. Defoe dispraises this faction as one of the two major dangerous "subdivided Parties" in the Harley administration (272). He notes that Harley was required to consolidate an autocratic single-party rule:

> They told him that it was Time to strike home, *as it was called*, at the whole Party; to give the Whigs the *Coup de Grace*, that they might die at once; to make a thorough Reformation, by displacing every Whig or Moderate Man in the Nation; to carry a *streight Rein*, and make the Government formidable, to restore the Prerogative, and make the People know their Duty [. . .]. (274)

In contrast, Defoe advocates the moderate maneuvers of Harley, who tried to "act only upon the Defensive" against, and display a conciliatory attitude toward, his political opponents:

> [H]e told them, They were to content themselves with reducing the Power of their Opposers, without turning Oppressors; [. . .] That they were to consider the Whigs as a part of the Queen's Subjects, who, though, they were to be restrained, were not to be oppress'd, much less destroy'd; That they struggled with the opposite Party to keep them from Tyrannizing, but were not to tyrannize in their stead. On the other hand, he told them, it was not their Part to push; that they were now *IN the Ministry*, and ought to risque nothing; their business was to preserve themselves in the Administration

where they were, and be satisfied with doing so [. . .]. (274–75)

Simply put, Defoe's strategy is to show up Harley's moderate character by reproving the hard-line actions of St John and extreme Tories, while he depicts Harley as "Master of the Plot," who "neither discovered himself one way or other, by which means the Politicians were effectually disappointed, the Attempt to sap the *White-Staff* and its Interest proved Abortive, and he yet held his hold, without receiving any Wound" (277–78). Given the fact that Harley was never viewed as having clean hands, Defoe accentuates his image as an adroit tightrope walker engaged in a political tug-of-war.

Another treacherous faction which Defoe warns against is made up of Jacobites, who "went with the [Harley] Ministry, in hopes of finding an Opportunity, out of the general Distractions, to produce something to the Advantage of that Party they adhered to, and to promote the Interest of the Pretender" (*Secret History* 272). Again he virtually accuses St John and his supporters of designing to interrupt the Protestant succession, which Harley had been committed to secure at the hazard of his political life. Defoe states that their aim was

> to trample under their Feet the Honour and Duty of Servants to the Queen, and the Principles of Respect and Gratitude to that superior Genius, who had formerly serv'd and obliged them in the highest Degree; and *which was yet worse*, to quit all that Regard which, as Ministers of State, they owed to the publick Good, and the Peace of their Country, which they well enough knew was centred in that one Capital Article of the Constitution, *viz.* The *Protestant Succession*. (282)

Giving advantage to the Pretender and Catholicism, which would contribute to the invasion by France, was considered extremely harmful to the maintenance of the national polity of Britain. Perhaps for that reason, in the closing part of the *Secret History*, Defoe denounces Francis Atterbury, Bishop of Rochester (1663–1732), for his Jacobitism as another "Chief Leader" of the opponents of the Harley ministry (293):[9]

> *Give away the Staff!* said the Bis— [Atterbury] By Lucifer I could not have believ'd she [Anne] durst have done it! What can we do without it, We have but one way left. *France* and the Lawful Heir [the Old Pretender]; it, must, and shall be done, By G—d. (294)

In this manner Defoe labels Harley's political adversaries en bloc as being "motivated by Jacobite sympathies" (Downie, Explanatory Notes 400n36), and emphasizes his efforts to protect the country by "do[ing] some publick Thing that would render the [Hanover] Succession Impregnable, past the Power of their Party to shake it, and out of Danger of being altered, whether the Queen should Live or Die" (Defoe, *Secret History* 283). Although Harley's actual scheme to deal with the Court of Hanover was not so amicable, Defoe tries to draw focus on the result that Harley fulfilled his role in thwarting Jacobite designs (Downie, Explanatory Notes 397, 399n21).

Defoe was unscrupulous enough to be suspected of already striking a bargain with the new Whig regime to write on its behalf, so we are allowed to be dubious about whether his political discourse reflects his true feelings. However, there is no doubt about his consistent endeavor in the *Secret History* to defend Harley by romanticizing his political behavior (Shiotani, *Daniel Defoe* 256–57, 260–68). For Defoe, it can be helpful for justifying his own literary activities and selling his capability as a political writer to his prospective employers at the same time.

About a month after the appearance of the *Secret History*, Swift wrote *Memoirs* at the request of nobody, unlike his many other partisan tracts. The fall of the Harley ministry compelled him to leave England, but even after the loss of the patronage of Tory politicians, he did not mean to convert to the Whig cause again. Instead, he aspired to become the Historiographer Royal "to write the official history" of Anne's reign, and he had actually "petitioned the Queen and the Earl of Oxford for the post and for the materials necessary for such a history," which ended in vain (Davis and Ehrenpreis xxxi). In fact, Bolingbroke took the trouble to recommend Swift for the position, writing to him: "'[T]is the Treasurers cause, 'tis my Cause, 'tis every mans cause who is embark'd in our bottom" ("Viscount Bolingbroke to Swift," *Correspondence* 1: 578; no. 259, [7 Jan. 1713–14]). Swift's own appeal for his appointment could embody his sense of mission to pass down a "correct" history of his time:

> The change of ministry about four years ago, [. . .] and the proceedings since, [. . .] are all capable of being very maliciously represented to posterity, if they should fall under the pen of some writer of the opposite party, as they probably may.
>
> Upon these reasons, it is necessary, for the honour of the Queen and in justice to her servants, that some able hand should be immediately employed to write the history of her Majesty's reign; that the truth of things may be transmitted to future ages, and bear down the falsehood of malicious pens.
>
> The Dean of St. Patrick's is ready to undertake this work, humbly desiring her Majesty will please to appoint him her historiographer, not from any view of profit, [. . .] but from an earnest desire to serve his Queen and country; for which that employment will qualify him, by an opportunity of access to those places where papers and records are kept, which will be necessary to any who undertake such an History. ("Dr. Swift's Memorial to

the Queen," *Correspondence* 1: 595; no. 269, 15 Apr. 1714)

Further, his pertinacity or near-obsession for being a witness of history (not exactly conducting the duties of the historiographer) amounted to a sarcastic remark directly to Harley — and indirectly to the Queen:

The Memory of one great Instance of your Candor and Justice, I will carry to my Grave; that having been in a manner domestick with you for almost four Years, it was never in the Power of any publick or concealed Enemy to make you think ill of me [. . .]. If I live, Posterity shall know that and more, which, though You, and somebody that shall be nameless [Anne], seem to value less than I could wish, is all the Return I can make You. Will you give me leave to say how I would desire to stand in Your Memory; As one who [. . .] never wilfully misrepresented Persons or Facts to you, nor consulted his Passions when he gave a Character. ("Swift to the Earl of Oxford," *Correspondence* 1: 628–29; no. 289, 3 July 1714)

Having failed to obtain the desired post, Swift was "obliged to depend on his own memory" to write *Memoirs* (Davis and Ehrenpreis xxxi), in which he persistently presents his complaint about the defeat of his hopes:

[T]his request proceed[ed] [. . .] from a sincere honest design of justifying the Queen, in the measures she then took, and after pursued, against a load of scandal which would certainly be thrown on her memory, with some appearance of truth. [. . .]

These were some of the arguments I often made use of with great freedom, both to the Earl of Oxford and my Lady Masham, to incite them to furnish me with materials for a fair account of that great transaction, to which they always seemed as well disposed as myself. My Lady Masham did likewise assure me, that she had frequently informed the Queen of my request, which her Majesty thought very reasonable [. . .].

But, that incurable disease, either of negligence or procrastination, which influenced every action both of the Queen and the Earl of Oxford, did in some sort infect every one who had credit or business in court: For, after soliciting near four years, [. . .] it was perpetually put off.

The scheme I offered was to write her Majesty's reign; and, that this work might not look officious or affected, I was ready to accept the historiographer's place [. . .].

This negligence in the Queen, the Earl of Oxford, and my Lady Masham, is the cause that I can give but an imperfect account of the first springs of that great change at court [. . .]. (*Memoirs, PW* 8: 109–10)

Thus it does not come as a surprise at all that *Memoirs* can reflect not only Swift's professional pride and historical consciousness to preserve an accurate record of the world of politics, independently of party backing, but also his emotional, as well as political and literary, rivalry with Defoe's *Secret History*. In the light of this context behind Swift, Defoe's choice of words in the title "*Secret History*" per se may have irritated him. At any rate, *Memoirs* was not intended for the manipulation of public opinion (Davis and Ehrenpreis xxx).

The first half of *Memoirs* is almost entirely devoted to explaining how and why the Godolphin administration broke down. In contrast to Defoe, Swift makes quite a brief reference to Sacheverell's trial: he simply concludes that it resulted from "a foolish passionate pique of the Earl of Godolphin" against sarcasm in Sacheverell's sermon (*PW* 8: 115). He does not feel the need to linger on the whole story about the case, possibly because for Swift, who professes himself a "High-churchman" (the same position as Sacheverell) within *Memoirs* (120), it is sufficient enough just to point out Godolphin's narrow-mindedness which culminated in his own and Harley's political advantage. Rather, he puts much greater weight on the detailed account of the blunders not only of Godolphin, but also of the Duke of Marlborough. As history shows, Anne gradually shifted her trust from the duumvirs to Harley. Swift catches the crucial moment of her change of mind, expounding on Harley's decisive advice to her as follows:

> He then told her of the dangers to her crown as well as to the church and monarchy itself, from the councils and actions of some of her servants: That she ought gradually to lessen the exorbitant power of the Duke and Duchess of Marlborough, and the Earl of Godolphin, by taking the disposition of employments into her own hands: That it did not become her to be a slave to a party; but to reward those who may deserve by their duty and loyalty, whether they were such as were called of the High or Low-church. In short, whatever views he had then in his own breast; or, how far soever he intended to proceed, the turn of his whole discourse was intended, in appearance, only to put the Queen upon what they called a moderating scheme; which however made so strong an impression upon her [. . .]. (116)

Regardless of the extent to which Swift reconstructs his original remarks, this can succinctly reflect the essence of Harley's politics and also display how well Swift understands and represents Harley's bipartisan political strategy. It seems as though he was continuing to make his talent appear both capable and useful, even though the tone of *Memoirs* is like that of a personal anecdote.

The latter half of *Memoirs* provides the description of how Swift began and developed his political and literary career, together with how he encountered Harley and how he was recruited as a ministerial propagandist. Here is the turning point of Swift's life where Harley talks Swift into wielding his pen for him:

> Mr. Harley told me, he and his friends knew very well what useful things I had written against the principles of the late discarded faction; and, that my personal esteem for several among them, would not make me a favourer of their cause: That there was now an entirely new scene: That the Queen was resolved to employ none but those who were friends to the constitution of church and state: That their great difficulty lay in the want of some good pen, to keep up the spirit raised in the people, to assert the principles, and justify the proceedings of the new ministers.
>
> [. . .] He added, That this province was in the hands of several persons, among whom some were too busy, and others too idle to pursue it; and concluded, that it should be his particular care, to establish me here in England, and represent me to the Queen as a person they could not be without. (Swift, *Memoirs*, *PW* 8: 123)

At the time, Defoe had already been "busy" working for Harley as a pamphleteer and spy (approximately from 1703 to 1714). With this somewhat extravagant flattery, Swift would seek to demonstrate that he establishes more intimate closeness to, and firmer confidence of, the new premier than Defoe did. Yet equally important is that Swift and Harley share the traditional values of the system of English government: the Anglican Church and the ancient constitution, that is, a mixed monarchy which holds the legislature of Crown, Lords, and Commons. Harley aims to protect this fundamental character of the nation, and Swift already advocated the concept in the *Discourse* in 1701. Hence Swift indirectly praises Harley's views of the "constitution of church and state" and the magnetism of his personality by claiming that he has achieved ideological consonance with the Earl from the very beginning, with a hint of contempt for Defoe's Presbyterian faith and his ability as a political writer.

In this context, what has often attracted academic attention in *Memoirs* is that there Swift defines his politico-religious position:

> I found myself much inclined to be what they called a Whig in politics; and [. . .] besides, I thought it impossible, upon any other principle, to defend or submit to the Revolution: But, as to religion, I confessed myself to be an High-churchman, and that I did not conceive how any one, who wore the habit of a clergyman, could be otherwise: That I had observed very well with what insolence and haughtiness some Lords of the High-church party treated not only their own chaplains, but all other clergymen whatsoever, and thought this was sufficiently recompensed by their professions of zeal to the church: That I had likewise observed how the Whig Lords took a direct contrary measure, treated the persons of partic- ular clergymen with great courtesy, but shewed much ill-will and contempt for the order in general: That I knew it was necessary for their party, to make their bottom as wide as they could, by taking all denominations of Protestants to be members of their body: That I would not enter into the mutual reproaches made by the violent men on either side; but, that the connivance, or encouragement, given by the Whigs to those writers of pamphlets, who reflected upon the whole body of the clergy, without any exception, would unite the church, as one man, to oppose them [. . .]. (*PW* 8: 120)

As a clergyman of the Church of Ireland having represented the "*Sentiments of a Church-of-England Man*," Swift makes it clear that he would never take a compromising attitude to Dissenters and the Whigs who are sympathetic with them. He adheres to the strength and stability of Anglicanism and the Established Church. As concerns his approbation of High Churchism, however, David Oakleaf points out that "[c]learly aware that popular opinion aligned the high-church position with the Tories, Swift nevertheless avoids calling himself a Tory" (38). Speck attempts to expound the intricacy of his religious sensibilities as follows:

> The likeliest explanation of Swift's anomalous role on the political stage of early eighteenth-century England is that he was a clergyman of the Church of Ireland. James II's policy of replacing Anglicans with Catholics in key position both in Church and State had gone much farther in Ireland than in England. [. . .] Thereafter there was absolutely no love lost between the Irish clergy and the hereditary Stuart line. [. . .] Their experiences had also given them a deeper hatred of the Catholics than was usual among the English clergy. At the same time the history of Ireland earlier in the seventeenth-century did little to endear them to the dissenters. [. . .] Hatred of what James II had done in Ireland turned the Irish clergy into Whigs. [. . .] On the other hand hatred of what papists and dissenters had done in Ireland turned them towards the Tories. [. . .]
>
> Swift shared the prejudices of the Irish clergy, and English politics therefore presented him with a real dilemma. Neither party both hated James II, the Catholic tyrant, and venerated Charles I, the Anglican martyr. ("From Principles to Practice" 81)

Swift could not place full confidence in the Tories, even though they generally belonged to the High-Church camp. He realized that both parties were carrying on their calculating schemes under the guise of piety. For him, the Established Church was not so much a mere citadel of faith as a fundamental political organ serving to unite the British people beyond all sects and to sustain Britain as the independent state under the rule of law, which could repel threats from outsiders — not only foreign powers, but also enemies at home.[10] In regard to Swift's political orientation, his self-definition as "a Whig in politics" cannot necessarily be taken in a literal sense. We should note his elaborate circumlocution in the passage cited above: he does not declare that he *is* a Whig; he "found" that his partisan inclination was leaning toward things that were generally "called" Whig in order to justify the Glorious Revolution, which forced James II to abdicate from the throne. On top of that, Swift openly criticizes the toleration policy of the Whigs. In view of his persistent espousal of the concept of mixed government, with a fairly conservative bent granting a power of arbitration to the king, irrespective of which party he supported, it can be fair to say that Swift intentionally conceals Tory elements, which are essentially more favorable to monarchism, in his political principles.[11] Actually, a few months before beginning to write *Memoirs*, he refers to the modification of the Tory ideology after the party's acceptance of William III in *Some Free Thoughts*:

> The Logick of the highest Tories is now, that this was the Establishment they found, as soon as they arrived to a Capacity of Judging; that they had no hand in turning out the late King, and therefore have no Crime to answer for, if it were any. That the Inheritance to the Crown is in pursuance of Laws made ever since their Remembrance, by which all Papists are excluded; and they have no other Rule to go by. That they will no more dispute King William the third's Title, than King William the first's; since they must have Recourse to History for both: That they have been instructed in the Doctrines of passive Obedience, Non-Resistance and Hereditary Right, and find them all necessary for preserving

the present Establishment in Church and State, and for continuing the Succession in the House of Hannover, and must in their own Opinion renounce all those Doctrines by setting up any other Title to the Crown. This I say, seems to be the Politicall Creed of all the high-principled Men, I have for some time met with of forty Years old, and under; which although I am far from justifying in every part, yet I am sure it sets the Protestant Succession upon a much firmer Foundation, than all the indigested Scheams of those who profess to act upon what they call Revolution-Principles. (*PW* 8: 92)

Although he is "far from justifying in every part" the *revised* Tory "Doctrines of passive Obedience, Non-Resistance and Hereditary Right," Swift is in basic agreement with them, while making a subtle dig at the Whiggish "Revolution-Principles." Given his persistent endeavor to vindicate the Revolution settlement and parliamentary control of the succession under stringent conditions, his advocacy of the ancient constitution can be seen as a clever synthesis of the actual stance of the Whigs and the concessional ideal of the Tories. With this sort of deliberate ambiguity about both church and state, Swift still tries to keep in step with Harley's middle-of-the-roadism. Such a strong presentation of his own political posture under the cloak of the defense of Harley's politics could vividly contrast with Defoe's relatively dispassionate-looking portrayal of the chief minister in the *Secret History*.[12]

As another noticeable difference from Defoe's discourse, we can point out that Swift shows off his personal contact with influential politicians as if he were privy — more privy than Defoe — to the inside affairs of the political world:

It was Mr. Harley's custom, every Saturday, that four or five of his most intimate friends, among those he had taken in upon the great change made at court, should dine at his house; and, after about two months acquaintance, I had the honour always to be one of the number. This company, at first, consisted only of the Lord-keeper Harcourt, the Earl Rivers, the Earl of Peterborow, Mr. Secretary St. John, and myself: And here, after dinner, they used to discourse, and settle matters of great importance. Several other Lords were afterwards, by degrees, admitted; as, the Dukes of Ormond, Shrewsbury, and Argyle; the Earls of Ailesbury, Dartmouth, and Powlet; the Lord Berkeley, &c. These meetings were always continued, [. . .] but, as they grew more numerous, became of less consequence; and ended only in drinking and general conversation [. . .].

My early appearance at these meetings, which many thought to be of greater consequence than really they were, could not be concealed, though I used all my endeavors to that purpose. (*Memoirs*, *PW* 8: 124)

At first glance, Swift appears to be humble himself, with the excuse that he joined the meetings of small merit and took pains to hide his attendance. However, this blatant self-deprecation, along with the excessive enumeration of the names of political figures, emphasizes the boastful demonstration of his political clout all the more effectively. Probably due to having a personal relationship with St John, Swift gives very little space in *Memoirs* to the criticism against him: he merely attributes the cause of the conflict between Harley and St John, which "afterwards had such unhappy consequences upon the publick affairs," to "youthful indiscretion in Mr. St. John" (128). Ironically, the reality was that Swift won less political confidence of the two than he naively assumed, though he "received consistently good-natured, spontaneous friendship from these great men" (Ehrenpreis 2: 585). Indeed he was convinced that he could converse with both of them on an equal footing,[13] declaring in the *Enquiry* that "these two great Men had hardly a common Friend left except my Self." He asserts that their friction "might very probably have been prevented if the Treasurer had dealt with less Reserve, or the Lord Bolingbroke had put that Confidence in Him which so sincere a Friend might reasonably have expected," and that their "Reconcilement" should not be "an Affair of much Difficulty" if he mediates between them (*PW* 8: 158; ch. 1). Nevertheless, despite his self-confidence and expectation, all his efforts to reconcile them eventually came to nothing.[14]

According to Ian Higgins, "Swift understood himself to be in great danger as a suspected Jacobite Tory" (*Swift's Politics* 18), but he delivers practically no attack on Jacobites in *Memoirs*. Provided that he was stimulated by the *Secret History*, it seems fairly likely that he could not possibly tolerate using the same logic as Defoe, who had shaken the society with his Dissenting views,[15] to tax St John with Jacobitism. Although Swift did not heartily vindicate or denounce St John, he would prefer his friendship with the Viscount to an open condemnation against his Jacobite inclination, so that he might insinuate Defoe's lack of inside knowledge of politics and politicians, exposing more grave apprehensions about Dissent than Jacobitism, in this case to level personal insults at Defoe.

In the words of Swift, Harley "assure[d] me very solemnly, That it was his opinion and desire, that no person should have the smallest employment, either civil or military, whose principles were not firm for the church and monarchy" (*Memoirs*, *PW* 8: 125). As we have seen, such conservative politico-religious values are the fundamental ties that bind Swift and Harley to serve for the security and stability of the country. Swift attached high priority to discharging his duties to support the Treasurer, rather than running the risk of fomenting internal discord within the Tories (by outspokenly censuring St John's machinations, for example). Compared with Defoe's partially fictional beautification of Harley's political actions, Swift's maneuver puts more weight on presenting an apparently historical account of Harley's and his own political commitment in unison to settling the confusion in party strife in the later Stuart period.

On the whole, if we pay close notice to Swift's self-respect for Anglican faith and political networking, we can perceive in *Memoirs* his intense sense of rivalry against Defoe and his *Secret History*. *Memoirs* might illustrate Swift's pride in his loyalty to conservative principles and in his management of human relations through an elaborate description of Harley's political attitudes. With its abundance of inside stories and political personages, *Memoirs* could even be better suited for the title "Secret History," which would paradoxically reveal the anticipated influence of Defoe on Swift. To put it another way, the *Secret History* is worth due critical attention to enrich our understanding of Swift's evaluation of Defoe's literary performance. It should be interesting to take a better look at Defoe's role as a precursor to Swift, not merely as a close competitor of him, and we can find of course a similar pattern in the relation of *Robinson Crusoe* and *Gulliver's Travels* in respect of the ideas on the British political framework.

4. *Gulliver's Travels* versus *Robinson Crusoe*: An Ideological Confrontation

Swift is thought to have begun writing *Gulliver's Travels* in 1721, and there is no doubt that, in order to create this literary magnum opus, he made the most of the material and experience with which he had written a number of political and historical documents (Davis and Ehrenpreis xxxix–lx). For instance, Gulliver's description of the political custom in Lilliput is quintessentially impressive:

In relating these and the following Laws, I would only be under-
stood to mean the original Institutions, and not the most scandalous
Corruptions into which these People are fallen by the degenerate
Nature of Man. For as to that infamaous Practice of acquiring great
Employments by dancing on the Ropes, or Badges of Favour and
Distinction by leaping over Sticks, and creeping under them; the
Reader is to observe, that they were first introduced by the Grand-
father of the Emperor now reigning; and grew to the present
Height, by the gradual Increase of Party and Faction. (*Gulliver's
Travels*, *PW* 11: 60; pt. 1, ch. 6)

Here we can feel déjà vu as the passage reminds us of the unproductive-
ness of party conflict which would lapse into corruption. It also satirizes
the "dirty" politics of Robert Walpole and the Whig supremacy under
the Hanoverian dynasty. In contrast, Brobdingnag is ranked as the most
preferable nation governed by human creatures, besides the country of
the Houyhnhnms, whose "rationality and order are not to be expected in
human life" (Lock, *Swift's Politics* 173).[16] Gulliver gives a relatively
positive assessment to its governing structure:

I was curious to know how this Prince, to whose Dominions
there is no Access from any other Country, came to think of Armies,
or to teach his People the Practice of military Discipline. But I was
soon informed, both by Conversation, and Reading their Histories.
For, in the Course of many Ages they have been troubled with the
same Disease, to which the whole Race of Mankind is Subject;
the Nobility often contending for Power, the People for Liberty,
and the King for absolute Dominion. All which, however happily
tempered by the Laws of that Kingdom, have been sometimes
violated by each of the three Parties; and have more than once
occasioned Civil Wars, the last whereof was happily put an End

to by this Prince's Grandfather in a general Composition; and the Militia then settled with common Consent hath been ever since kept in the strictest Duty. (Swift, *Gulliver's Travels*, *PW* 11: 138; pt. 2, ch. 7)

Brobdingnag at present is ruled by a wise and principled king, and, based on the reflection on the past power struggle between Crown, Lords, and Commons culminating in "Civil Wars," the check and balance system which can control the three powers of government is now in operation. This can symbolize a sound function of mixed monarchy, specifically a romanticized version under the later Stuarts, established after the chaos of the Puritan and Glorious Revolutions. Swift must have intended to starkly compare the political situations of Lilliput and Brobdingnag because in both countries critical changes occurred *coincidentally* in the same age — in the reign of the grandfather of the current prince. By this means he nostalgically extols the reign of Queen Anne, which gave him glory days as a political agent and pamphleteer, and undermines the image of George and the Walpole administration.

About two years before the start of writing *Gulliver's Travels* appeared *Robinson Crusoe*, whose presence Swift could never have been unconscious of, and onto which Defoe can project part of his vision of the state. After getting accustomed to the self-sufficient life on the deserted island, Crusoe falls into a pleasant reverie of being an absolute monarch:

It would have made a Stoick smile to have seen, me and my little Family sit down to Dinner; there was my Majesty the Prince and Lord of the whole Island; I had the Lives of all my Subjects at my absolute Command. I could hang, draw, give Liberty, and take it away, and no Rebels among all my Subjects.

Then to see how like a King I din'd too all alone, attended by

> my Servants, *Poll*, as if he had been my Favourite, was the only Person permitted to talk to me. My Dog who was now grown very old and crazy, and had found no Species to multiply his Kind upon, sat always at my Right Hand, and two Cats, one on one Side the Table, and one on the other, expecting now and then a Bit from my Hand, as a Mark of special Favour. (*Robinson Crusoe* 166)

Crusoe can fully exercise his unlimited power to spare or to kill over his subjects, but they are just small animals that cannot resist the powerful king. In view of Defoe's Dissenting background, such a seemingly ludicrous description of the image of the Crown may mock the despotic inclination of a Catholic monarch like James II. Later, after saving the lives of Friday's father and a Spaniard, Crusoe again blows his own trumpet about ruling his "country," now human-populated, as the supreme sovereign:

> My Island was now peopled, and I thought my self very rich in Subjects; and it was a merry Reflection which I frequently made, How like a King I look'd. First of all, the whole Country was my own meer Property; so that I had an undoubted Right of Dominion. *2dly*, My People were perfectly subjected: I was absolute Lord and Lawgiver; they all owed their Lives to me, and were ready to lay down their Lives, *if there had been Occasion of it*, for me. It was remarkable too, we had but three Subjects, and they were of three different Religions. My Man *Friday* was a Protestant, his Father was a *Pagan* and a *Cannibal*, and the *Spaniard* was a Papist: However, I allow'd Liberty of Conscience throughout my Dominions [. . .]. (235)

This time Defoe puts an emphasis on the autocrat, with absolute dominion over his human citizens, exhibiting religious toleration. Generally this passage could allow two interpretations: the one is that it indicates the Declarations of Indulgence, which were originally intended for giving official approval to Catholics, but were at the same time Charles II's and James II's attempts to enlist Dissenters into their cause; the other is that it admires the leadership of William III, who could be regarded as the protector of Dissenting worship coming from overseas. However, if we approach this delineation from the viewpoint of Swift, Anglican clergyman with a sense of rivalry and disgust with Defoe, it may display a cynical disrespect for Anglicanism. Look at the position of the three subjects: faithful Friday is a Protestant (perhaps a Dissenter[17]) placed on the first and the *left* of the sentence; the nameless and somehow mysterious Spaniard is a Catholic on the *right*; in the meantime, Friday's father, the most barbarous placed *between* the two, is "a *Pagan* and a *Cannibal*," which could possibly imply that the Church of England, theoretically standing between Protestantism and Catholicism, unjustly threatens nonconforming faith with a violent wielding of authority.

Concerning Defoe's political thought, Manuel Schonhorn admits: "That Daniel Defoe was a strong supporter all his life of England's constitutional monarchy and her mixed government, and particularly, of William III and the Revolution of 1689, cannot be denied" (161). At one time Defoe put a premium on the voice of the people, even above king and parliament if they go against public interest, but he basically approved of a limited monarchy, trying to keep his distance from both the theory of the divine right of kings and the theory of social contract and to find the rhetoric that can mediate the contrasting concepts to justify the Revolution settlement (Hayashi 161, 164, 261–69; Takeda, "Meiyo-kakumei" 321–38). On the face of it, Swift could possibly have sought common ground with Defoe's politics, but he must never have accepted its liberal nature and, above all, his unreserved mockery of Anglicanism, the power and status of the Crown, and the Stuart reign — all of which were treasures of Swift's theory and political life. For

Swift, therefore, Defoe was not just his literary rival, but an ideological polemicist who inflamed his conservative desire. Thus the concept of mixed monarchy, which can be literarily utilized in *Gulliver's Travels*, is supposed to work as an efficient rhetorical countermeasure against imaginary enemies to Swift's political and religious ideals, even in his dark days after being thrown out of the center of English political circles.

5. Summary: From Politics via History to Literature — Swift's Ideological Efforts on the Eve of the *Travels*

In the last analysis, Swift was a committed disputant who, with moderation in mind, tried to hybridize the principles on both sides in order to set an ideal that would go beyond the bounds of party ideology. Rather than being a hired moderate propagandist, he was quite extreme in his determination to defend and maintain the national polity with his conservative values, though not given to extremes in policy itself. His equivocal stance may appear to be opportunistic, but he was consistent in his political principles regardless of the changes of the ruling party. Since his unpublished papers were written in the decline, or after the fall, of the Harley ministry, he could have availed himself of the opportunities to ingratiate himself with the Whigs and Walpole or to deliver a fatal blow to Harley and St John, if he had been so minded. The keynote of his argument, however, had not changed at all from that of his former Tory (or, further back, even Whig) tracts, in point of his skepticism about the effectiveness of the dual party system and his rejection of all forms of faith but Anglicanism as heresy.

Compared with Defoe, Swift had a strong pride as a (would-be) historiographer who was versed in the "secret history" of politics and politicians. Despite his political career being ruined at the start of the

Hanoverian period, Swift endeavored to save face and keep on expressing his conservative ideals under the guise of historical records. It is quite likely that Defoe's works stirred him to champion the political and religious dispensation especially during Anne's reign (though in a glorifying manner), and he made good use of his experience as a political (and possibly historical) writer and also of the rhetoric of the theory of the ancient constitution to construct *Gulliver's Travels*.

Conclusion

In this study, we have seen that Swift's politico-religious ideology, elaborately presented in his English writings in the late Stuart to early Hanoverian period, had a striking consistency in upholding the stability of the Anglican establishment, the protection of Protestant sovereigns, and, not least, the proper maintenance of the mixed monarchy. Regardless of his change of party affiliation, the conservative drift of his argument remained unchanged from his debut as a political writer with the publication of *A Discourse of the Contests and Dissensions in Athens and Rome*, and we can recognize that the political rhetoric of his journalistic discourse was efficaciously applied even in the making of *Gulliver's Travels*.

Now that we could reveal a distinctive character of Swift's political thought, we should venture to explain his standpoint always in dispute. It is certain that Ian Higgins's Jacobite reading of his politics is highly effective in comprehending his firm High-Church bent and his relative sympathy toward the Stuart dynasty. However, it must be at variance with his continued championship of the Revolution settlement, along with his theoretical efforts to acknowledge the abdication of James II, deny the legitimacy of the Pretender, and justify the accession of William III. As for the Whig interpretation as typified by J. A. Downie, it does serve for appreciating Swift's self-declaration as "a Whig in politics" (*Memoirs*, PW 8: 120), but it faces a major challenge from a reasonable assumption that Swift was not exactly an ardent supporter of social contract. Rather, it is plain that he had regular recourse to the concept of the ancient constitution to bolster his political contention, especially placing a high priority on the royal authority as the arbiter between the three powers of Crown, Lords, and Commons. Meanwhile, the Tory interpretation as represented by F. P. Lock is considerably valid in accounting for Swift's pursuit of conservative values. Nevertheless, it is worth noting that, although Swift recognized the hereditary right to the throne as a standing rule, he admitted the control of the royal succession by the rule of law if driven to necessity. Strictly speaking, it was concessively modified Tory principles that he gave countenance to in order to secure the Protestant succession, and he saw as the ideal political structure parliamentary government which must be operated compatibly with the monarchical constitution. He never abandoned Whiggish principles: he advocated a *limited* monarchy and granted the people's right of resistance if the king acts "directly contrary to the Laws he hath consented to, and sworn to maintain" (*Examiner*, *PW* 3: 114; no. 33, 22 Mar. 1710–11).

In the face of such intricate inexplicability, a conservative reading of Swift's works can provide a practical effectiveness, or rather, convenience, in subsuming the conflicting views on his political and literary performance. Indeed Swift definitely converted from Whig to Tory, but his ideological conviction was invariably constant, not exactly labeled as being neutral or moderate, but based on the tradition of conservatism — and the politics of this nature has historical and remarkable precedents in his past and present. The three supposed "trimmers" — Marquess of Halifax, Robert Harley, and our man, Swift — have in common the consistent reliance on the theory of mixed monarchy and the function of the Church of England to some degree or another, while their allegiance to party has constantly been questioned. Their motive was to seek and assure the maintenance of social order in the unstable period when there was always fear of drastic social change, that is, war (either civil or foreign) or revolution, and they actually contributed to the protection of traditional English national polity called the ancient constitution. After due consideration of their politics, we can safely state that the trimmer is not a mere political weathercock; to put it more precisely, his political action (choice of party) appears to be opportunistic, but his political thought (choice of principle) is consistent in holding conservative beliefs that can avoid going into extremism — which could be proposed as a new definition of "trimmer" in the context of the political situation under the later Stuarts.

Oddly enough, so far there has been no direct reference to Halifax found in Swift's writings. His name does not appear in the index of *The Prose Writings of Jonathan Swift* (vol. 14), or in the list of Swift's library when we consult *The Library and Reading of Jonathan Swift: A Bio-Bibliographical Handbook*, the astonishing fruit of Dirk F. Passmann and Heinz J. Vienken's amazingly extensive research. However, as the present study has shown, if we consider the history of the theory of mixed government, it is quite unnatural to conclude that Swift knew nothing about the thoughts and actions of Halifax, a key player behind the scenes in the late seventeenth century. In fact, to take the case of *A Tale of a Tub*, the author plainly shows deep involvement in religious and political matters at the time, picking up *"Exclusion Bills,"* as well as *"Popish Plots," "Passive Obedience," "Prerogative,"* and *"Liberty of Conscience"* (*PW* 1: 42; sec. 1, introduction). These topics infallibly attracted Swift's attention, and he could never have ignored Halifax's role as the Trimmer. Later in *An Argument against Abolishing Christianity in England*, we can find a plausible usage of the word, "trimmer":

> Are Party and Faction rooted in Mens Hearts no deeper than Phrases borrowed from Religion; or founded upon no firmer Principles? And is our Language so poor, that we cannot find other Terms to express them? [. . .] [I]s our Invention so barren, we can find no others? Suppose, for Argument Sake, that the *Tories* favoured *Margarita*, the *Whigs* Mrs. *Tofts*, and the *Trimmers Valentini*; would not *Margaritians*, *Toftians*, and *Valentinians*, be very tolerable Marks of Distinction? (*PW* 2: 32)

Here the "*Trimmers*" are treated as persons independent of, or at least separate from, the Tory-Whig dichotomy. It does not necessarily mean that they take a neutral stand; they would rather advance their unique or sometimes prejudiced opinions to settle the case. Now it is fairly reasonable to suppose that we can put Swift in the same category with Halifax, or possibly and hopefully in the imaginary line of "conservative" trimmers.

All things considered, Swift, a notable political writer under the Harley administration, can be equally qualified to appear on the list of the history of conservative thought, if Halifax occupies a position in that sphere as Anthony Quinton offers. The author of the *Tale* "writ under three Reigns," and declares his hope after retirement, which is to work on "Speculations more becoming a *Philosopher*" (*PW* 1: 42; sec. 1, introduction; emphasis added). Consciously or unconsciously, Swift wrote on politics substantially "under three Reigns" — William III, Anne, and George I — and actually his ideological efforts poured into his politico-religious writings throughout the most of his literary career make him duly deserve to be called a thinker.

While there has been considerable research which deals with Swift's politics, it would be expected that this study could promote a better understanding of his rhetorical and theoretical techniques for conveying to the public his ideals, whether political or religious, through his various literary products. If we seek to conduct a fuller evaluation of his achievements as a publicist, a careful perusal of his Irish writings will be of significant help. From this point we might go on to redraw the whole picture of his life and works, which would also serve to enhance the exploration of the English — or preferably British — way of conservative intellectual history.

Notes

Introduction

1 For another concise and fair summary of this interpretative history of Swift's political slant, see Oakleaf 35–36.

2 Quinton presents two more "specific principles" of conservatism. One is "organicism," which sees a society as "a unitary, natural growth, an organized, living whole, not a mechanical aggregate," constituted not by "bare abstract individuals," but by "social beings, related to one another within a texture of inherited customs and institutions which endow them with their specific social nature" (16). To meet this condition, we would point to Swift's adherence to "common forms," as Ann Cline Kelly postulates in connection with his views on the English language (Nakajima, "Riron" 5–6):

> Enriched for generations, traditional English expresses the time-tested verities of British civilization, which Swift called the common forms. As the persisting elements of culture, the common forms provide a historical structure that binds men together and makes their lives meaningful. Without common forms, barbarity reigns, and so Swift devoted his energies to preserving cultural fixtures such as the Established Church, the constitutional monarchy, and the English language. (Kelly 10)

> [T]he "common Forms" represent the stabilizing expectations of the group that control the disruptive or domineering impulses of the individual. These cultural forms, including the English Language, have evolved over time and transcended particular places and persons. They have become permanent elements of civilized life. (11)

For a further discussion on Swift's opinion of the stability of the English language and British civilization, see Nakajima, "Jonathan Swift." The other principle of conservatism is "political skepticism," which advances "the belief that political wisdom, the kind of knowledge that is needed for the successful management of human affairs, is not to be found in the theoretical speculations of isolated thinkers but in the historically accumulated social experience of the community as a whole" (Quinton 16–17). Swift's association with this factor could be endorsed by his dispraise of Hobbesian views of society and his respect for inherited Anglican establishment, as will be seen in chapter 2. For the sake of my argument in this book, I should put a premium on traditionalism, which is presumed to be most relevant to the issue of national polity, and to which Quinton himself attaches the highest importance (see note 4).

3 In the light of the tradition of the polity of England, this governing structure is regarded as almost equivalent to the so-called ancient constitution, which is composed of Crown, Lords, and Commons (Dickinson 62–64).

4 Quinton insists that conservatism is based on "a belief in the imperfection of human nature" both religious and secular. The imperfection has two aspects: "intellectual and moral." He goes on to explain:

> The consequence of men's intellectual imperfection is that they should not conduct their political affairs under the impulsion of large, abstract projects of change arrived at by individual thinkers working in isolation from the practical realities of political life. They should be guided rather by the accumulated political wisdom of the community. The consequence of men's moral imperfection is that men, acting on their own uncontrolled impulses, will on the whole act badly, however elevated their professed intentions may be. They need, therefore, the restraint of customary and established laws and institutions, of an objective and impersonal barrier to the dangerous extravagance of subjective, personal impulse. (13)

According to his argument, "[t]he two imperfections converge, from different directions, on the first, traditionalist principle, the most important of the three" (18). Incidentally, although Quinton lays more weight on the intellectual side (13), we will need to keep in mind that Swift was highly sensitive to the depravity of human morality and cast severe reflections on corruption in politics (see chapter 3, section 3). Also in this respect, we could say that Swift had an innate aptitude for leaning toward conservatism.

Chapter 1

1 The other three impeached were William Bentinck, 1st Earl of Portland (1649–1709); Edward Russell, Earl of Orford (1652–1727); and Charles Montagu, 1st Earl of Halifax (1661–1715), who was 1st Baron Halifax at the time (Nishiyama, "Matthew Prior" 208–10).

2 Davis, Introduction, Swift, *PW* 1: xix–xx; Goldie 31–32; Hashinuma 63.

3 See chapter 4, note 4.

4 Swift shows the process for falling into tyranny and its fate as below:

> [I]n order to preserve the Ballance in a mixed State, the Limits of Power deposited with each Party ought to be ascertained, and generally known. The Defect of this is the Cause that introduces those Strugglings in a State about *Prerogative* and *Liberty*, about Encroachments of the *Few*, upon the Rights of the *Many*, and of the *Many* upon the Privileges of the *Few*; which ever did, and ever will conclude in a Tyranny; First, either of the *Few*, or the *Many*, but at last infallibly of a single Person. (*Discourse*, *PW* 1: 200–01; ch. 1)

Usually, "*Prerogative*" and "*Liberty*" are vested respectively in the "*Few*" and the "*Many*" as their essential right. In this context, the "*Few*" would definitely mean the nobles, and the "*Many*" the commons.

5 Swift sees Solon (c. 630–c. 560 BC) as the supposed founder of an ideal system of governance in Athens (*Discourse*, *PW* 1: 204–05; ch. 2).

6 As mentioned above, the tyranny of the people is doomed to end up in that of one man, so, for Swift, the populace is considered foolish enough to make vain efforts toward the monopoly of power, being used almost as a tool for the ruler:

> [A]lthough most Revolutions of Government in *Greece* and *Rome* began with the Tyranny of the People, yet they generally concluded in that of a single Person. So that an usurping Populace is its own *Dupe*; a meer Underworker, and a Purchaser in Trust for some single Tyrant; whose State and Power they advance to their own Ruin, with as blind an Instinct, as those Worms that die with weaving magnificent Habits for Beings of a superior Nature to their own. (*Discourse*, *PW* 1: 227; ch. 4)

This much he looks down on, or is at least skeptical about, the credibility on democratic government.

7 Cited below are the lessons from Rome which Swift takes. We can observe his condensed distrust of the political ability of the common people.

> *First*, [. . .] when the Ballance of Power is duly fixed in a State, nothing is more dangerous and unwise than to give way to the *first Steps* of Popular Encroachments [. . .]. If there could one single Example be brought from the whole Compass of History, of any one popular Assembly, who after

beginning to contend for Power, ever sat down quietly with a certain Share: Or if one Instance could be produced of a popular Assembly, that ever knew, or proposed, or declared what Share of Power was their due; then might there be some Hopes that it were a Matter to be adjusted by Reasonings, by Conferences, or Debates: But since all that is manifestly otherwise, I see no other Course to be taken in a settled State, than a steady constant Resolution in those to whom the rest of the Ballance is entrusted, never to give Way so far to popular Clamours, as to make the least Breach in the Constitution [. . .].

Again, [. . .] it will not be difficult to gather and assign certain Marks of popular Encroachments; by observing of which, those who hold the Ballance in a State, may judge of the Degrees, and by early Remedies and Application, put a Stop to the fatal Consequences that would otherwise ensue. [. . .]

Another Consequence is this, That (with all Respect for popular Assemblies be it spoke) it is hard to recollect one Folly, Infirmity or Vice, to which a single Man is subjected, and from which a Body of Commons either collective or represented can be wholly exempt. For, besides that they are composed of Men with all their Infirmities about them; they have also the ill Fortune to be generally led and influenced by the very worst among themselves; I mean, *Popular Orators*, *Tribunes*, or, as they are now stiled, *Great Speakers*, *Leading Men*, and the like. (*Discourse*, *PW* 1: 226–27; ch. 4)

8 Kenyon, Introduction 12–15; Yamaguchi 46; Yamasaki and Yamaguchi 145–54.

9 The Saviles were a prestigious and rich family (Kenyon, Introduction 7; Raleigh xi–xii; Reed 47–48), so there was no need for Halifax to pursue his personal success.

10 The *Character* gained "wild popularity," and "went through at least three editions in 1689 alone" (Pincus 589n95). It was also posthumously issued five times by 1717 (Yamaguchi 56n5).

11 Halifax in his young days "spent several years abroad, mainly Huguenot south of France — and he retained a strong sympathy for republicanism to the end" (Kenyon, Introduction 7). See also Reed 47; Yamasaki and Yamaguchi 138–39.

12 G. P. Gooch argues that if Halifax "had a fault as a thinker, it was that he scarcely realized the reserves of wisdom and sanity latent in the average unlettered citizen" (155). See also Yamaguchi 46, 53–54. It should be noted, however, that British society (especially the majority of the Whigs, who can be considered

progressive) did not choose a genuine democratic system of government even at the time of the Glorious Revolution. In contemporary political circles, men of property were the most trustworthy, and it was not uncommon to make light of, or even fear, the people seizing political power. Actually, social revolution was not that welcomed by the rank and fashion (Dickinson 57–62).

13 Swift also laid stress on morality as an indispensable part of a man of power (see chapter 3, section 3). Swift and Halifax have something in common in respect to political stance (Raleigh ix–x), and there should be the possibility of treating Swift as a "Trimmer," possibly together with Godolphin and Harley, both of whom formed a coalition government between the two parties after the Glorious Revolution (Yamaguchi 56, 56–57n6).

14 For a detailed discussion on Hooker's elaborate middle-of-the-roadism between the royal authority and the consent of the people, see Nakajima, "Richard Hooker."

15 Greenberg 194–95; Kawamura 4–5; Weston 26–27.

16 Kawamura 8; Pocock 309; Weston 10–11.

17 As to the degenerated condition of government, the *Answer* describes as follows: "The ill of absolute Monarchy is Tyranny, the ill of Aristocracy is Faction and Division, the ills of Democracy are Tumults, Violence and Licentiousnesse" (*ANP* 263).

18 See also Kawamura 20–21.

19 According to Janelle Greenberg, "[p]ublished with his [Charles I's] seal in at least seven editions, the *Answer* reached an ever-widening audience with this message: sovereignty now vested not in the monarch alone but in that holy trinity of law-makers, King, Lords, and Commons. And this on the word of a king" (196).

Chapter 2

1 For an incisive discussion on Swift's criticism against Hobbes's concept of modern state, see Nishiyama, *Jonathan Swift* 244–54.

2 In actuality, Hobbes raised a contemporary suspicion that he was an atheist because his peculiar religious beliefs in *Leviathan* offended, and made enemies out of, various sects. To which denomination, particularly either Anglican or Independent, he gave countenance is still an open question (Sommerville 365–66; Springborg, "Hobbes" 346–47; Tuck 34–39, 97).

3 In *A Project for the Advancement of Religion, and the Reformation of Manners*, written in the year following the *Argument*, Swift reiterates such a claim:

142

[I]f Religion were once understood to be the necessary Step to Favour and
Preferment; can it be imagined, that any Man would openly offend against it,
who had the least Regard for his Reputation or his Fortune? There is no
Quality so contrary to any Nature, which Men cannot affect, and put on upon
Occasion, in order to serve an Interest, or gratify a prevailing Passion: The
proudest Man will personate Humility, the morosest learn to flatter, the
laziest will be sedulous and active, where he is in pursuit of what he hath
much at Heart: How ready therefore would most Men be to step into the
Paths of Virtue and Piety, if they infallibly led to Favour and Fortune? (*PW*
2: 50)

[I]t should be thought, that the making Religion a necessary Step to Interest
and Favour, might encrease Hypocrisy among us: And I readily believe it
would. But if One in Twenty should be brought over to true Piety by this, or
the like Methods, and the other Nineteen be only Hypocrites, the Advantage
would still be great. Besides, Hypocrisy is much more eligible than open
Infidelity and Vice: It wears the Livery of Religion, it acknowledgeth her
Authority, and is cautious of giving a Scandal. Nay, a long continued
Disguise is too great a Constraint upon human Nature, especially an *English*
Disposition. Men would leave off their Vices out of meer Weariness, rather
than undergo the Toil and Hazard, and perhaps Expence of practising them
perpetually in private. And, I believe, it is often with Religion as it is with
Love; which, by much Dissembling, at last grows real. (56–57)

It looks as if Swift encourages practical attitude to religion, but, as he is acutely
aware of human imperfection, his focus would be put on exerting all possible effort
to avoid repealing the Test Act and protect the Anglican Church system. Instead of
risking a head-on confrontation with nonconformists (and the Whigs who support
them) that could provoke strong opposition, he proposes in an ironic manner the
need for a thorough (not an *occasional*) "Disguise," which could possibly end up
in maintaining *real* Anglican faith.

    4 In this pamphlet, Swift is supposed to be critically conscious of Daniel
Defoe's *An Essay upon Projects* (1697): "Among all the Schemes offered to the
Publick in this projecting Age, I have observed, with some Displeasure, that there
have never been any for the Improvement of Religion and Morals" (*Project, PW* 2:
44). This could also reflect Swift's anti-Dissenting intent to advocate Anglican
ecclesiastical order. In *A Letter from a Member of the House of Commons in
Ireland to a Member of the House of Commons in England, concerning the*

Sacramental Test (1708), the innuendo against Defoe is more direct: he is described as "the Fellow that was *pilloryed*, I have forgot his Name," who "is indeed so grave, sententious, dogmatical a Rogue, that there is no enduring him" (*PW* 2: 113). The tract champions the Church of Ireland and castigates Presbyterians and Catholics. The following is an example of the reprobation against the latter sect, which would invite a foreign menace:

> *Popery* is now the *common Enemy*, against which we must all unite: I have been tired in History with perpetual Folly of those States, who called in Foreigners to assist them against a *common Enemy*: But the Mischief was, these *Allies* would never be brought to allow that the *common Enemy* was quite subdued: And they had Reason; for it proved at last, that one Part of the *common Enemy* was those who called them in; and so the *Allies* became at length the *Masters*. (121–22)

As to the former, Swift criticizes its unlimited demand for toleration:

> When I was a Boy, I often heard the *Presbyterians* complain, that they were not permitted to serve God in their own Way; they said, they did not repine at our Employments, but thought that all Men, who live peaceably, ought to have Liberty of Conscience, and Leave to assemble. That Impediment being removed at the Revolution, they soon learned to swallow the *Sacramental Test*, and began to take very large Steps, wherein all who offered to oppose them, were called Men of a *persecuting Spirit*. During the time the Bill against Occasional Conformity was on Foot, *Persecution* was every Day rung in our Ears, and now at last the *Sacramental Test* it self has the same Name. (122)

Levelling such bidirectional accusations, this *Letter* works as a warning to the Whigs in power to prevent the repeal of the Test Act in Ireland, which would undermine the stability of the Church and the country itself (Davis, Introduction, Swift, *PW* 2: xxii).

5 Such sense of worth is later wrought into *Gulliver's Travels*. Look at the adoption standard for political jobs in Lilliput:

> In chusing Persons for all Employments, they have more Regard to good Morals than to great Abilities: For, since Government is necessary to Mankind, they believe that the common Size of human Understandings, is

fitted to some Station or other; and that Providence never intended to make the Management of publick Affairs a Mystery, to be comprehended only by a few Persons of sublime Genius, of which there seldom are three born in an Age: But, they suppose Truth, Justice, Temperance, and the like, to be in every Man's Power; the Practice of which Virtues, assisted by Experience and a good Intention, would qualify any Man for the Service of his Country, except where a Course of Study is required. But they thought the Want of Moral Virtues was so far from being supplied by superior Endowments of the Mind, that Employments could never be put into such dangerous Hands as those of Persons so qualified; and at least, that the Mistakes committed by Ignorance in a virtuous Disposition, would never be of such fatal Consequence to the Publick Weal, as the Practices of a Man, whose Inclinations led him to be corrupt, and had great Abilities to manage, to multiply, and defend his Corruptions.

In like Manner, the Disbelief of a Divine Providence renders a Man uncapable of holding any publick Station: For, since Kings avow themselves to be the Deputies of Providence, the *Lilliputians* think nothing can be more absurd than for a Prince to employ such Men as disown the Authority under which he acteth. (*Gulliver's Travels*, *PW* 11: 59–60; pt. 1, ch. 6)

"Moral Virtues" are placed ahead of professional abilities. In addition, established faith and the king's status as the head of religion are confirmed in the constitution of Lilliput. This portrayal seems to claim the legitimacy of the Church of England and the Test Act in the real world.

6 The "state of nature" which Hobbes presents to us is the one where men can resort to violence to secure their own self-preservation (88–90; pt. 1, ch. 13).

7 Hobbes even approves of thought control over the people by the ruler (Tuck 84–85). In *Leviathan*, he maintains:

[I]t is annexed to the Soveraignty, to be Judge of what Opinions and Doctrines are averse, and what conducing to Peace; and consequently, on what occasions, how farre, and what, men are to be trusted withall, in speaking to Multitudes of people; and who shall examine the Doctrines of all bookes before they be published. For the Actions of men proceed from their Opinions; and in the wel governing of Opinions, consisteth the well governing of mens Actions, in order to their Peace, and Concord. And though in matter of Doctrine, nothing ought to be regarded but the Truth; yet this is not repugnant to regulating of the same by Peace. For Doctrine repugnant to Peace, can no more be True, than Peace and Concord can be against the Law of Nature. [. . .] It belongeth therefore to him that hath the Soveraign Power, to be Judge, or constitute all Judges of Opinions and Doctrines, as a thing necessary to Peace; thereby to prevent Discord and Civill Warre. (124–25; pt. 2, ch. 18)

We can sense his deep-rooted suspicion of the discretion of the people. The "wel governing" of popular opinion is considered an effective measure against "Discord and Civill Warre" of the nation.

8 Ryan 235; Skinner 171–72.

Chapter 3

1 Dickinson 91–95, 121–25. Plumb states: "After 1715, power could not be achieved through party and so the rage of party gave way to the pursuit of place" (189). Once the strife between the two parties was settled into the Whig one-party domination, making use of patronage, a political method analogous to the spoils system, became much more crucial for the seizure of power.

2 See also Speck, *Stability and Strife* 4–5.

3 The change of dynasty from Stuart to Hanover brought about a change of government, but the noted first ministers of each reign (Godolphin and Harley in the former, and Walpole in the latter) had a common strategy, that is, managing politics by controlling patronage.

4 Nonetheless, historical scholarship has always been updated, and research is conducted to rediscover modernity which deserves to be called a "revolution" in the interpretation of the Glorious Revolution, such as Steve Pincus's *1688: The First Modern Revolution*. For a useful and detailed survey of the studies on the history of the Revolution, see Sakashita.

5 J. A. Downie points out that Harley expected to prevent the "High Church reaction" from "[obscuring] the moderate principles on which he hoped to found the new ministry" at the "tory resurrection" around 1710. His aim in appointing Swift as a leading ministerial propagandist was "to influence public opinion," "to maintain the 'spirit' of moderation and unity," and

to try to reconcile the country gentlemen to the real nature of the regime envisaged by the prime minister, much in the same way that Defoe, through the *Review*, was at the time trying to convince the whigs and monied men that out and out High-Flying administration was not the desire of the new ministers. (*Robert Harley* 128)

The main audience of Swift's Tory pamphlets consisted of the Tory country gentlemen and the provincial clergy (Cook 53; Downie, *Robert Harley* 138; Lock, "Swift and English Politics" 134), and Swift was "much more interested in attacking his enemies than in proselytizing them" (Cook 53). Richard I. Cook insists:

> Swift's moderation, [. . .] though he no doubt thought of it as such, is actually more apparent than real in those tracts he wrote for contemporary publication. [. . .] Philosophically Swift's position, whatever his contentions, was not a happy middleground between two extremes — he was much closer to the October Club in his sympathies than he was to any dedicated Whig. In the bulk of his pamphlets he is seldom even mildly critical of the most reactionary Tories, while Whigs, however moderate, come under blistering attack. (49)

Conversely, however, it would be possible to say that by analyzing these Tory-biased pamphlets we can perceive the degree to which "Whiggish" elements could be introduced that might be acceptable even to the Tory readers.

6 The following passage from *The Examiner* no. 35 (5 Apr. 1711) will help to illustrate Swift's stance on party allegiance and to endorse Cook's analysis:

> If these two Rivals [Whig and Tory] were really no more than *Parties*, according to the common Acceptation of the Word; I should agree with those Politicians who think, a Prince descendeth from his Dignity by putting himself at the Head of either; and that his wisest Course is, to keep them in a Balance; raising or depressing either, as it best suited with his Designs. But, when the visible Interest of his Crown and Kingdom lies on one Side; and when the other is but a *Faction*, raised and strengthened by Incidents and Intrigues, and by deceiving the People with false Representations of Things; he ought, in Prudence, to take the first Opportunity of opening his Subjects Eyes, and declaring himself in favour of those, who are for preserving the Civil and Religious Rights of the Nation, wherewith his own are so inter-woven. (*PW* 3: 122)

Such sense of balance between the king and the two parties seems to share some common traits with that between the three powers of mixed government (Crown, Lords, and Commons), which Swift associated with the image of scales, granting administrative priority to the Crown, in the *Discourse* (see chapter 1, section 1). At the individual level, the Tories were considered "the party which best embodies" Swift's beliefs for the moment (Cook 38), and the Whigs before Harley's grip on power.

7 Swift writes affirmatively in *Examiner* no. 33 (22 Mar. 1710–11) as a Tory tenet: "[A] supream, absolute, unlimited Power [. . .] is lodged in the King or Queen, together with the Lords and Commons of the Kingdom" (*PW* 3: 113). He also admits that "a free People" can "lawfully resist" an "arbitrary King" if his "Commands [. . .] are directly contrary to the Laws he hath consented to, and sworn to maintain," and that laws should "limit the Prerogative," which can lead to the deterrence of tyranny (113–14).

8 In principle, the basis of the constitution such as kingship and fundamental law is indefeasible, but Swift accepts that they are allowed to be modified if the parliament sanctions:

> As to the Succession; the *Tories* think an *Hereditary Right* to be the best in its own Nature, and most agreeable to our old Constitution; yet at the same Time they allow it to be defeasible by Act of Parliament; and so is *Magna Charta* too, if the Legislature think fit; which is a Truth so manifest, that no Man who understands the Nature of Government, can be in doubt concerning it. (*Examiner*, *PW* 3: 114; no. 33)

In the *Conduct*, he also refers to the changeability of succession, which must have stirred up an argument:

> It is certainly for the Safety and Interest of the *States-General*, that the Protestant Succession should be preserved in *England*; because such a Popish Prince as we apprehend, would infallibly join with *France* in the Ruin of that Republick. [. . .] Her Majesty is in the full peaceable Possession of Her Kingdoms, and of the Hearts of Her People; among whom, hardly one in five hundred are in the *Pretender*'s Interest. [. . .] Neither perhaps is it right, in point of Policy or good Sense, that a Foreign Power should be called in to confirm our Succession by way of Guarantee; but only to acknowledge it. Otherwise we put it out of the Power of our own Legislature to change our Succession, without the Consent of that Prince or State who is Guarantee; however our Posterity may hereafter, by the Tyranny and Oppression of any

succeeding Princes, be reduced to the fatal Necessity of breaking in upon the excellent and happy Settlement now in force. (*PW* 6: 27)

In the postscript of the *Conduct*, added to its fourth edition, he supplements as follows:

> I put a distant Case of the possibility that our *Succession*, through extream Necessity, might be changed by the Legislature, in future Ages; and it is pleasant to hear those People quarrelling at this, who profess themselves for changing it as often as they please, and that even without the Consent of the entire Legislature. (65)

He notes down "fatal Necessity" in the body of the work, and here he imposes the condition that there must be an "extream Necessity" and the "Consent of the entire Legislature" when intervening in the line of succession. He dares to adopt such rhetoric to emphasize over and over that the abdication of James II and the elimination of the Pretender were caused due to unavoidable circumstances. These statements can prove that, in order to prevent the rule of "a Popish Prince," Swift went to such lengths to justify the accession of William III and the Revolution settlement, even if he was not very positive about them, and that he was clearly in favor of parliamentary politics under the reign of a Protestant monarch.

9 See *Examiner* no. 16 (23 Nov. 1710).

10 They are supposedly nos. 16, 20 (21 Dec. 1710), and 27 (8 Feb. 1710–11).

11 Harley criticizes the political extravagance of Godolphin and the Marlboroughs "[i]n court, in ye Revenue, in the camp" respectively at length as follows (104):

> In the court none must appear but their sworne vassals. This they openly avowe & herein they place their security not regarding that Parliam[ts.] have always censored the Highest monopoly as the most criminal. Thus the chiefest places of Profit & Trust are shared by the family; they let their vassals have nothing that they can keep themselves or give to their own kindred. Whoever stands in their way must be removed at any expence. As for those they suffer to come in, with some they divide the Profits, but all must profess an unlimited obedience to all their commands. (104–05)

> Turne yr eyes to the Public Revenue. [. . .] Even the Civil List will produce a *Debt* that will startle him [my honest Countryman] while a

multitude of the greatest & most preferred Offices and Pensions together with the privy Purse *are* engrossed at Home, and an uninhabitable Palace is erecting. [. . .] The necessary services of ye nation will be left as a debt upon you while that money is diverted to private use, & those who have the Public Purse, & no faith of their own, are Bountiful corrupters of other mens Truth: I could point out Bargains of great profit made & confined to their creatures when more advantageous offers for ye Public have been refused. What should I name selling of Places, which is so common that every chairman knows it and the Brokers who act therein. In short necessary services are starved to enrich an overgrown family. (105)

If you look into the camp; there you will see a scene of disorder, Factions fomented and discipline neglected: not serving well, but flattery, and mean submissions are the road to advancement. (106)

12 The Harley family, espousing Presbyterianism and radical Whiggism for three generations, criticized the pro-Catholic policies by James and welcomed the accession of William and Mary (Matsuzono 175–76), though Downie defines the Earl of Oxford as "a whig with a dissenting background" but "in essence [. . .] a High Churchman" like Swift to maintain that they were "two of a rare kind" in the contemporary political circles (*Robert Harley* 128).

Chapter 4

1 Swift himself suggests in the *Enquiry* that he already wrote before it "two severall Treatises, of which the One is an History, and the other Memoirs of particular Facts" to defend the conduct of the Harley ministry. At the same time, he admits that "neither of them [are] fit to see the Light at present, because they abound with Characters freely drawn, and many of them not very amiable; and therefore intended only for the Instructing of the next Age, and establishing the Reputation of those who have been usefull to their Country in the present" (*PW* 8: 141; ch. 1). In actuality, all the three drafts ended up being published posthumously.

2 F. P. Lock, too, recognizes: "Apart from its vigorous (though hardly historical) character sketches, the most interesting passages in the *History* are those that expound Swift's own ideas" ("Swift and English Politics" 142).

3 First, Swift voices an objection to the naturalization law for foreign Protestants:

> [T]he Act for naturalizing Foreign Protestants [. . .] had been contrived under the last Ministry; and, as many People thought, to very evil Purposes. By this Act any Foreigner, who would take the Oaths to the Government, and profess himself a Protestant of whatever Denomination, was immediately Naturalized; and had all the Priviledges of an *English*-born Subject at the expence of a Schilling. Most Protestants abroad differ from Us in the Point of Church Government; so that all the Acquisitions by this Act would encrease the Number of Dissenters; and therefore the Proposal that such Foreigners should be obliged to conform to the Established Worship, was rejected. (*History*, *PW* 7: 94)

He recognizes the uniqueness of the Anglican "Established Worship" system, and foreigners are identified with Dissenters due to their difficulty in conforming to it. Subsequently, he snaps at Presbyterians in Scotland:

> [T]he Act [was] passed to prevent the Disturbing those of the Episcopal Communion in *Scotland*, in the Exercise of their Religious Worship, and in the Use of the Liturgy of the Church of *England*. It is known enough, That the most considerable of the Nobility and Gentry there, as well as great Numbers of the People, dread the Tyrannical Discipline of those Synods and Presbyteries; and, at the same time have the utmost Contempt for the Abilities and Tenets of their Teachers. It was besides thought an Inequality beyond all appearance of Reason or Justice, That Dissenters of every Denomination here, who are the Meanest and most Illiterate Part among us, should possess a Toleration by Law, under colour of which they might upon occasion be bold enough to insult the Religion established; while those of the Episcopal Church in *Scotland* groaned under a real Persecution. (96)

Here Swift again shows open animosity to "Dissenters of every Denomination," pointing to the concern that the Anglican episcopacy is at stake in the country where Presbyterianism is prevailing. Lastly, he points the finger at Quakers:

> The Sect of Quakers among us, whose System of Religion first founded upon Enthusiasm hath been many years grown into a Craft, held it an unlawful Action to take an Oath to a Magistrate. This Doctrine was taught them by the Author of their Sect, from a literal Application of the Text, *Swear not at all*. But being a Body of People wholly turned to Trade and Commerce of all kind, they found themselves on many Occasions deprived

of the Benefit of the Law, as well as of Voting at Elections by a foolish Scruple, which their Obstinacy would not suffer them to get over. To prevent this Inconvenience, these People had Credit enough in the late Reign, to have an Act passed, That their Solemn Affirmation and Declaration should be accepted instead of an Oath in the usual Form. The great Endeavour in those Times was to lay all Religion upon a Level [. . .]. (106)

Swift maliciously describes Quakers as impious bargainers who have sold their souls for business. To such an extent he becomes religiously sensitive enough to launch an all-out attack on nonconformity, possibly on the grounds of the enactment of the Occasional Conformity Act (1711–19).

4 As he never approves of a civil revolution, Swift does not necessarily support pure democracy. He rather seems to be disposed to oligarchy. In *Examiner* no. 40 (10 May 1711), he recognizes the merit of birth:

I cannot but take Notice, That of all the Heresies in Politicks, profusely scattered by the Partisans of the *late Administration*, none ever displeased me more, or seemed to have more dangerous Consequences to *Monarchy*, than that pernicious Talent so much affected, of discovering a Contempt for *Birth*, *Family*, and *ancient Nobility*. [. . .] Most popular Commotions we read of in Histories of *Greece* and *Rome*, took their Rise from unjust Quarrels to the *Nobles*; and in the latter, the *Plebeians* Encroachments on the *Patricians*, were the first Cause of their Ruin.

Suppose there be nothing but *Opinion* in the Difference of Blood; every Body knows, that *Authority* is very much founded on *Opinion*. But surely, that Difference is not wholly imaginary. The Advantages of a liberal Education, of chusing the best Companions to converse with; not being under the Necessity of practicing little mean Tricks by a scanty Allowance; the enlarging of Thought, and acquiring the Knowledge of Men and Things by Travel; the Example of Ancestors inciting to great and good Actions. These are usually some of the Opportunities that fall in the Way of those who are born, of what we call the better Families; and, allowing *Genius* to be equal in them and the Vulgar, the Odds are clearly on their Side. Nay, we may observe in some, who by the Appearance of Merit, or Favour of Fortune, have risen to great Stations, from an obscure Birth, that they have still retained some sordid Vices of their *Parentage* or *Education*, either *insatiable Avarice*, or *ignominious Falshood* and *Corruption*. (*PW* 3: 150)

The rhetoric Swift uses here overlaps with that in the *Discourse*, where he attributes the collapse of ancient states to the gradual encroachment of commoners upon the power and privilege of aristocrats, repeating the term "*Dominatio Plebis*" (see chapter 1, section 1). It is also noticeable that he expects the benefit of gentle blood to prevent avarice, which he thinks is a chief adverse factor for being an incorruptible politician (see chapter 3, section 3). Lock gives us an effective explanation for Swift's preference of the propertied class as follows:

> Swift's ideal political order is hierarchical, based on the exercise of power and influence by a mainly hereditary class whose inherited wealth and social position gives them a natural right to determine public policies. [. . .] He advances several reasons for believing that nobility confers real benefits and advantages. These are the superior education and culture to which it gives (or it ought to give) access; the examples of noble ancestors to emulate; and the political virtue that comes from having property to defend. In the tradition of the classical republicans, Swift thought that political power was best entrusted to those who had a real stake in their country. For, being already wealthy, they would not easily be bribed to betray the national interest which was also their own. (*Swift's Tory Politics* 174–75)

5　As to the expression "White Staff," it is "an emblem of the office of Lord Treasurer" (Downie, Explanatory Notes 400n34).

6　In this regard, Swift's *Gulliver's Travels* obviously parodies and mocks Defoe's *Robinson Crusoe*. For example, at the opening of the former, Gulliver introduces himself as "the Third of five Sons" of a middle-class family (*Gulliver's Travels, PW* 11: 19; pt. 1, ch. 1). The setting of the protagonist is the same as the latter: also at its front, Crusoe identifies himself as "the third Son of the Family" in "the middle State, or what might be called the upper Station of Low Life" (*Robinson Crusoe* 57, 58). See Higgins, Explanatory Notes 287; Swift, *Gulliver's Travels, CE* 15: 29n2; Takeda, Kaisetsu 466–68.

7　Maximillian E. Novak conjectures that "[i]t is possible that Defoe was still receiving some secret remuneration from Harley" to publish the *Secret History* (36).

8　Downie, *Robert Harley* 185–88; Novak 36; Shiotani, *Daniel Defoe* 252–54.

9　The Lord Chancellor, Simon Harcourt, 1st Viscount Harcourt (c. 1661–1727), was also named and cursed at as a "Chief Leader" (Defoe, *Secret History* 293–94), although he was a local and political friend of Harley's "until drawn into the Bolingbroke camp at the end of the reign of Queen Anne" (Downie, Explanatory

Notes 400n31). According to Downie, Defoe seems to suggest that "Harcourt, rather than Bolingbroke, is *the* 'Chief Leader' of the faction opposed to Oxford," but "there is no evidence for his assertion" and his motive (Explanatory Notes 400n34; emphasis added). Certainly Harcourt was a Tory, but whether he was a Jacobite or not is not yet satisfactorily proved.

10   Speck observes: "Metaphysical sanctions [. . .] Swift considered to be absolutely necessary to preserve morality in civil society. He was also persuaded that the State should back them up with the discipline of a State Church" ("From Principles to Practice" 78). The Established Church can be conceived of as being indispensable to support the maintenance of political order from a spiritual aspect.

11   Although I do not wholly agree with his adamant insistence on Swift's Jacobite inclination, there is considerable validity in the argument by Ian Higgins. He claims:

> There are cogent reasons why Swift did not call himself a Tory. 'Tory' in Ireland implied Jacobite. [. . .] In a political atmosphere where 'Tory' signified Jacobite, Swift and Pope, periodically accused of Jacobitism, called themselves Whigs, yet Swift was expected to be sympathetic to a reputed Jacobite. (*Swift's Politics* 23–24)

This "atmosphere" could encourage Swift to disguise the tinge of Toryism in his writings after the Hanoverian succession.

12   One of the most plausible reasons why Defoe did not spout off about his own political conviction in the *Secret History* is that he already made a secret promise with the coming Whig administration, as already mentioned.

13   Swift boldly wrote to Harley, who was about to fall from power:

> When I was with you I have said more than once, that I would never allow Quality or Station made any reall Difference between Men. Being now absent and forgotten, I have changed my Mind. [. . .] [I]n your publick Capacity you have often angred me to the Heart, but as a private man never once. So that if I onely lookt towards my self I could wish you a private Man to morrow. [. . .] I will never write to you (if I can help it) otherwise than as to a private Person, nor allow my self to have been obliged by You in any other Capacity. [. . .] I will add one thing more, which is the highest Compliment I can make, that I never was afraid of offending You, nor am now in any Pain for the manner I write to You in. ("Swift to the Earl of Oxford," *Correspondence* 1: 628–29; no. 289)

To Bolingbroke, shortly after the death of Queen Anne, he showed a self-reliant attitude as a professional writer:

> All I pretended was, to speak my thoughts freely, to represent persons and things without any mingle of my interest or passions, and, sometimes, to make use of an evil instrument [the pen or the press], which was like to cost me dear, even from those for whose service it was employed. ("Swift to Viscount Bolingbroke," *Correspondence* 2: 57; no. 343, 7 Aug. 1714)

Even though such remarks might be his display of bravado, Swift strove to build a personal friendship with the charismatic leading politicians of the day, through which he seems to take pride in his self-assurance as a man and an author.

14 Here are Swift's explanations of his unsuccessful mediation between the ministers. In a letter to Bolingbroke, he says:

> I said to him [my Lord Oxford], that, upon the foot your Lordship and he then were, it was impossible you could serve together two months [. . .]. I am only sorry, that it was not a resignation, rather than a removal; because the personal kindness and distinction I always received from his Lordship and you, gave me such a love for you both, [. . .] that I resolved to preserve it entire, however you differed between yourselves; and in this I did, for some time, follow your commands and example. I imputed it more to the candour of each of you, than to my own conduct; that, having been, for two years, almost the only man who went between you, I never observed the least alteration in either of your countenances towards me. [. . .] When I saw all reconciliation impracticable, I thought fit to retire; and was resolved, for some reasons (not to be mentioned at this distance) to have nothing to do with whoever was to be last in. For, either I should not be needed, or not be made use of. And let the case be what it should, I had rather be out of the way. ("Swift to Viscount Bolingbroke," *Correspondence* 2: 56–57; no. 343)

Nearly a year later, Swift writes in the *Enquiry*:

> I had managed between them for almost two Years; and their Candour was so great, that they had not the least Jealousy or Suspicion of me. And I thought I had done Wonders, when upon the Queen's being last at Windsor, I put them in a Coach to go thither by Appointment without other Company; where they would have four Hours Time to come to a good Understanding;

But in two days after, I learned from them Both, that nothing was done. (*PW* 8: 158–59; ch. 1)

15 Defoe was arrested, imprisoned, and pilloried for publishing the seditious libel, *The Shortest Way with the Dissenters* (1702).

16 In the last chapter of *Gulliver's Travels*, Swift makes Gulliver praise morality in Brobdingnagian politics as the model which can be followed by the "corrupt" humans:

> [W]ho can read of the Virtues [. . .] in the glorious *Houyhnhnms*, without being ashamed of his own Vices, when he considers himself as the reasoning, governing Animal of his Country? I shall say nothing of those remote Nations where *Yahoos* preside; amongst which the least corrupted are the *Brobdingnagians*, whose wise Maxims in Morality and Government, it would be our Happiness to observe. (*PW* 11: 292; pt. 4, ch. 12)

17 Protestants can include Anglicans in principle, but in this case the possibility seems unlikely. It is conjectured that Presbyterian Defoe would make a distinct contrast between the Catholic Spaniard and non-Catholic Friday, whose character he shapes as remarkably loyal and pious.

Works Consulted

青柳かおり『イングランド国教会——包括と寛容の時代』彩流社、2008 年。
(Aoyagi, Kaori. *England-kokkyo-kai: Hokatsu to kan'yo no jidai* [*Comprehension and Toleration: The Church of England under the Later Stuarts*]. Sairyusha, 2008. In Japanese.)

Ashcraft, Richard. *Locke's Two Treatises of Government.* Unwin Hyman, 1987. Unwin Critical Library.

Burgess, Glenn. *Absolute Monarchy and the Stuart Constitution.* Yale UP, 1996.

——. *The Politics of the Ancient Constitution: An Introduction to English Political Thought, 1603–1642.* Pennsylvania State UP, 1993.

[Charles I]. "Extracts from *His Majesties Answer to the XIX. Propositions of Both Houses of Parliament.*" Weston, pp. 261–65.

[——]. "The King's Answer to the Nineteen Propositions, 18 June 1642." Kenyon, *Stuart Constitution*, pp. 18–20.

Cook, Richard I. *Jonathan Swift as a Tory Pamphleteer.* U of Washington P, 1967.

Curley, Edwin. "Hobbes and the Cause of Religious Toleration." Springborg, *Cambridge Companion*, pp. 309–34.

Davis, Herbert. Introduction. Swift, *PW*, vol. 1, pp. ix–xxxvi.

——. Introduction. Swift, *PW*, vol. 2, pp. ix–lx.

——. Introduction. Swift, *PW*, vol. 3, pp. ix–xxxv.

Davis, Herbert, and Irvin Ehrenpreis. Introduction. Swift, *PW*, vol. 8, pp. ix–xl.

Defoe, Daniel. *The Life and Strange Surprizing Adventures of Robinson Crusoe (1719).* Edited by W. R. Owens, 2008. *The Novels of Daniel Defoe*, general editors, W. R. Owens and P. N. Furbank, vol. 1, Pickering and Chatto, 2008–09. 10 vols. The Pickering Masters: The Works of Daniel Defoe.

——. *Party Politics.* Edited by J. A. Downie, 2000. *Political and Economic Writings of Daniel Defoe*, general editors, W. R. Owens and P. N. Furbank, vol. 2, Pickering and Chatto, 2000. 8 vols. The Pickering Masters: The Works of Daniel Defoe.

——. *Robinson Crusoe.* Edited by Thomas Keymer, notes by Thomas Keymer and James Kelly, Oxford UP, 2007. Oxford World's Classics.

——. *The Secret History of the White-Staff (1714).* Defoe, *Party Politics*, pp. 263–94.

Dickinson, H. T. *Liberty and Property: Political Ideology in Eighteenth-Century Britain.* 1977. Methuen, 1979. University Paperbacks 678.

Downie, J. A. Explanatory Notes. Defoe, *Party Politics*, pp. 373–406.

——. *Jonathan Swift: Political Writer*. Routledge and Kegan Paul, 1984.

——. *Robert Harley and the Press: Propaganda and Public Opinion in the Age of Swift and Defoe*. Cambridge UP, 1979.

Ehrenpreis, Irvin. *Swift: The Man, His Works, and the Age*. Methuen, 1962–83. 3 vols.

Filmer, Robert. *Patriarcha and Other Writings*. Edited by Johann P. Sommerville, Cambridge UP, 1991. Cambridge Texts in the History of Political Thought.

Finn, Stephen J. *Hobbes: A Guide for the Perplexed*. Continuum, 2007. Guides for the Perplexed.

Foxcroft, H. C. *The Life and Letters of Sir George Savile, Bart., First Marquis of Halifax &c.: With a New Edition of His Works, Now for the First Time Collected and Revised*. Longmans, Green, and Co., 1898. 2 vols.

Furbank, P. N., and W. R. Owens. *A Critical Bibliography of Daniel Defoe*. 1998. Pickering and Chatto, 2000.

Goldie, Mark. "Situating Swift's Politics in 1701." Rawson, pp. 31–51.

Gooch, G. P. *Political Thought in England: Bacon to Halifax*. Geoffrey Cumberlege, 1915. Home University Library of Modern Knowledge 96.

Greenberg, Janelle. *The Radical Face of the Ancient Constitution: St. Edward's "Laws" in Early Modern Political Thought*. 2001. Cambridge UP, 2006.

[Harley, Robert]. "Plaine English to All Who Are Honest or Would Be So If They Knew How: A Tract by Robert Harley." Edited by W. A. Speck and J. A. Downie. *Literature and History*, no. 3, 1976, pp. 100–10.

橋沼克美「『桶物語』の政治的意義」『言語文化』、42 巻、2005 年、61–75 頁。 (Hashinuma, Katsumi. "*Oke-monogatari* no seiji-teki-igi" ["Political Significance of Swift's *A Tale of a Tub*"]. *Gengo bunka* [*Cultura Philologica*], vol. 42, 2005, pp. 61–75. In Japanese.)

林直樹『デフォーとイングランド啓蒙』京都大学学術出版会、2012 年　プリミエ・コレクション 19。 (Hayashi, Naoki. *Defoe to England keimo* [*Daniel Defoe and the English Enlightenment*]. Kyoto UP, 2012. Premiere Collection 19. In Japanese.)

Higgins, Ian. Explanatory Notes. Swift, *Gulliver's Travels*, edited by Claude Rawson, pp. 278–362.

——. "Jonathan Swift's Political Confession." Rawson, pp. 3–30.

——. *Swift's Politics: A Study in Disaffection*. Cambridge UP, 1994. Cambridge Studies in Eighteenth-Century English Literature and Thought 20.

Hobbes, Thomas. *Leviathan*. Edited by Richard Tuck, rev. student ed., Cambridge UP, 1996. Cambridge Texts in the History of Political Thought.

岩井淳 (Iwai, Jun.)『ピューリタン革命の世界史――国際関係のなかの千年王国論』

ミネルヴァ書房、2015 年　MINERVA 西洋史ライブラリー 105（静岡大学人文社会科学部研究叢書 47）。(*Puritan-kakumei no sekai-shi: Kokusai-kankei no naka no sennen-okoku-ron* [*A Euro-American History of the Puritan Revolution: Millenarianism in International Relations*]. Minerva Shobo, 2015. Minerva seiyo-shi library [Minerva Occidental History Library] 105 (Shizuoka daigaku jimbun-shakai-kagaku-bu kenkyu-sosho [Research Publication Series of the Faculty of Humanities and Social Sciences, Shizuoka U] 47). In Japanese.)

――.『ピューリタン革命と複合国家』山川出版社、2010 年　世界史リブレット 115。(*Puritan-kakumei to fukugo-kokka* [*The Puritan Revolution and the British Composite State*]. Yamakawa Shuppansha, 2010. Sekai-shi librétto [World History Librétto] 115. In Japanese.)

川村大膳「議会派十九ヵ条提案に対するチャールズ一世の『解答』について――十七世紀混合政府論の起源と系譜」『人文論究』、17 巻、4 号、1967 年、1–22 頁。(Kawamura, Daizen. "Gikai-ha-jukyu-kajo-teian ni taisuru Charles-issei no *Kaito* ni tsuite: Junana-seiki-kongo-seifu-ron no kigen to keifu" ["On Charles I's *Answer* to the Nineteen Propositions: The Origin and Genealogy of the Seventeenth-Century Theory of Mixed Government"]. *Jimbun ronkyu* [*Humanities Review*], vol. 17, no. 4, 1967, pp. 1–22. In Japanese.)

Kelly, Ann Cline. *Swift and the English Language*. U of Pennsylvania P, 1988.

Kenyon, J. P. Introduction. Savile, *Halifax*, pp. 7–39.

――. *Revolution Principles: The Politics of Party, 1689–1720*. (The Ford Lectures: 1975–6.) 1977. Cambridge UP, 1990. Cambridge Studies in the History and Theory of Politics.

――, editor. *The Stuart Constitution, 1603–1688: Documents and Commentary*. 2nd ed., Cambridge UP, 1986.

小林章夫『スコットランドの聖なる石――ひとつの国が消えたとき』日本放送出版協会、2001 年　NHK ブックス 918。(Kobayashi, Akio. *Scotland no seinaru ishi: Hitotsu no kuni ga kieta toki* [*Scotland's Stone of Scone: A Brief History of the Disappearance of a Country*]. NHK, 2001. NHK Books 918. In Japanese.)

Lock, F. P. "Swift and English Politics, 1701–14." *The Character of Swift's Satire: A Revised Focus*, edited by Claude Rawson, U of Delaware P, 1983, pp. 127–50.

――. *Swift's Tory Politics*. Duckworth, 1983.

Locke, John. *Two Treatises of Government*. Edited by Peter Laslett, student ed., Cambridge UP, 1988. Cambridge Texts in the History of Political Thought.

松園伸『イギリス議会政治の形成――「最初の政党時代」を中心に』早稲田大学出版部、1994 年。(Matsuzono, Shin. *Igirisu-gikai-seiji no keisei: "Saisho no seito-jidai" wo chushin ni* [*The Formation of British Parliamentary Government: A Focus on the "First Age of Party"*]. Waseda UP, 1994. In Japanese.)

中島渉 (Nakajima, Wataru.)「ジョナサン・スウィフトの英語改革案が持つ文化的意図」『上智英語文学研究』、26 号、2001 年、35–46 頁。("Jonathan Swift no eigo-kaikaku-an ga motsu bunka-teki-ito" ["The Cultural Intention of Jonathan Swift's *Proposal* for Correcting the English Language"]. *Sophia English Studies*, no. 26, 2001, pp. 35–46. In Japanese.)

——. "Richard Hooker as a Moderator of Political Ideology: The Duality of His Via Media Philosophy in *Of the Laws of Ecclesiastical Polity*." *Asterisk*, vol. 13, 2004, pp. 17–30.

——.「理論と実際の埋めがたき溝──スウィフトの道徳的政治観と馬の国」『上智英語文学研究』、31 号、2006 年、3–15 頁。("Riron to jissai no umegataki mizo: Swift no dotoku-teki-seiji-kan to uma no kuni" ["The Unbridgeable Gap between Theory and Practice: Jonathan Swift's Moral Politics and Houyhnhnmland"]. *Sophia English Studies*, no. 31, 2006, pp. 3–15. In Japanese.)

——. "Thomas Hobbes's Advocacy of Monarchy: An Inquiry into His Views on the National Constitution in *Leviathan*." *Asterisk*, vol. 17, 2008, pp. 21–34.

"The Nineteen Propositions, 1 June 1642." Kenyon, *Stuart Constitution*, pp. 222–26.

西山徹 (Nishiyama, Toru.)『ジョナサン・スウィフトと重商主義』岡山商科大学、2004 年　岡山商科大学学術研究叢書 6。(*Jonathan Swift to jusho-shugi* [*Jonathan Swift and Mercantilism*]. Okayama Shoka U, 2004. Okayama shoka daigaku gakujutsu-kenkyu-sosho [Okayama Shoka U Academic Publication Series] 6. In Japanese.)

——.「マシュー・プライアー造反の理──詩人外交官の相対的世界」冨樫、207–59 頁。("Matthew Prior zohan no ri: Shijin-gaikokan no sotai-teki-sekai" ["Matthew Prior's Reasons for Defection: The Relative World of a Poet-Diplomat"]. Togashi, pp. 207–59. In Japanese.)

Novak, Maximillian E. "Defoe's Political and Religious Journalism." *The Cambridge Companion to Daniel Defoe*, edited by John Richetti, Cambridge UP, 2008, pp. 25–44. Cambridge Companions to Literature.

Oakleaf, David. "Politics and History." *The Cambridge Companion to Jonathan Swift*, edited by Christopher Fox, Cambridge UP, 2003, pp. 31–47. Cambridge Companions to Literature.

[Parker, Henry?]. *A Political Catechism*. Weston, pp. 267–79.

Passmann, Dirk F., and Heinz J. Vienken. *The Library and Reading of Jonathan Swift: A Bio-Bibliographical Handbook; Part 1, Swift's Library in Four Volumes*. Peter Lang, 2003. 4 vols.

Pincus, Steve. *1688: The First Modern Revolution*. Yale UP, 2009. The Lewis Walpole Series in Eighteenth-Century Culture and History.

Plumb, J. H. *The Growth of Political Stability in England, 1675–1725*. Macmillan P, 1967.

Pocock, J. G. A. *The Ancient Constitution and the Feudal Law: A Study of English Historical Thought in the Seventeenth Century; A Reissue with A Retrospect*. Cambridge UP, 1987.

Polybius. *The Histories: Books 5–8*. 1923. Translated by W. R. Paton, revised by Frank W. Walbank and Christian Habicht, 2nd ed., Harvard UP, 2011. Loeb Classical Library 138.

Quinton, Anthony. *The Politics of Imperfection: The Religious and Secular Traditions of Conservative Thought in England from Hooker to Oakeshott*. Faber and Faber, 1978. T. S. Eliot Memorial Lectures Delivered at the U of Kent at Canterbury in Oct. 1976.

Raleigh, Walter. Introduction. Savile, *Complete Works*, pp. vii–xxviii.

Rawson, Claude, editor. *Politics and Literature in the Age of Swift: English and Irish Perspectives*. Cambridge UP, 2010.

Reed, A. W. "George Savile, Marquis of Halifax." *The Social and Political Ideas of Some English Thinkers of the Augustan Age, A. D. 1650–1750: A Series of Lectures Delivered at King's College, University of London during the Session 1927–28*, 1923, edited by F. J. C. Hearnshaw, Greenwood P, 1983, pp. 47–68.

Ryan, Alan. "Hobbes's Political Philosophy." Sorell, pp. 208–45.

坂下史「名誉革命史と『言説空間』の位置——政治、文学、公共圏」冨樫、17–64 頁。(Sakashita, Chikashi. "Meiyo-kakumei-shi to 'gensetsu-kukan' no ichi: Seiji, bungaku, kokyo-ken" ["The History of the Glorious Revolution and the Positioning of the 'Sphere of Discourse': Politics, Literature, and Public Sphere"]. Togashi, pp. 17–64. In Japanese.)

[Savile, George]. *The Complete Works of George Savile, First Marquess of Halifax*, edited by Walter Raleigh, Clarendon P, 1912.

[——]. *Halifax: Complete Works*. Edited by J. P. Kenyon, Penguin Books, 1969. Pelican Classics.

[——]. *The Works of George Savile, Marquis of Halifax*. Edited by Mark N. Brown, vol. 1, Clarendon P, 1989. 3 vols.

Schonhorn, Manuel. *Defoe's Politics: Parliament, Power, Kingship, and* Robinson Crusoe. Cambridge UP, 1991. Cambridge Studies in Eighteenth-Century English Literature and Thought 9.

塩谷清人 (Shiotani, Kiyoto.)『ダニエル・デフォーの世界』世界思想社、2011 年。(*Daniel Defoe no sekai* [*The World of Daniel Defoe*]. Sekaishisosha, 2011. In

Japanese.)

——.『ジョナサン・スウィフトの生涯——自由を愛した男』彩流社、2016 年。
(*Jonathan Swift no shogai: Jiyu wo aishita otoko* [*The Life of Jonathan Swift: The Man Who Loved Liberty*]. Sairyusha, 2016. In Japanese.)

Skinner, Quentin. "Hobbes on Persons, Authors and Representatives." Springborg, *Cambridge Companion*, pp. 157–80.

Sommerville, Johann. "*Leviathan* and Its Anglican Context." Springborg, *Cambridge Companion*, pp. 358–74.

Sorell, Tom, editor. *The Cambridge Companion to Hobbes*. Cambridge UP, 1996. Cambridge Companions to Philosophy.

Speck, W. A. "From Principles to Practice: Swift and Party Politics." *The World of Jonathan Swift: Essays for the Tercentenary*, edited by Brian Vickers, Harvard UP, 1968, pp. 69–86.

——. *Stability and Strife: England, 1714–1760*. Harvard UP, 1977. The New History of England.

Speck, W. A., and J. A. Downie. Introductory Note. Harley, pp. 100–02.

Springborg, Patricia, editor. *The Cambridge Companion to Hobbes's* Leviathan. Cambridge UP, 2007. Cambridge Companions to Philosophy.

——. "Hobbes on Religion." Sorell, pp. 346–80.

[St John, Henry]. *Bolingbroke's Defence of the Treaty of Utrecht: Being Letters VI–VIII of* The Study and Use of History. Introduction by G. M. Trevelyan, Cambridge UP, 1932.

[——]. *A Letter to the Examiner*. Swift, *PW*, vol. 3, pp. 219–27.

Swift, Jonathan. *An Argument to Prove, That the Abolishing of Christianity in England, May, as Things Now Stand, Be Attended with Some Inconveniences, and Perhaps, Not Produce Those Many Good Effects Proposed Thereby*. 1711. Edited by Herbert Davis. Swift, *PW*, vol. 2, pp. 26–39.

——. *The Cambridge Edition of the Works of Jonathan Swift*. General editors, Claude Rawson et al., Cambridge UP, 2008– . 6 vols. to date [of 17 vols. projected].

——. *The Conduct of the Allies*. 1711. Edited by Bertrand A. Goldgar and Ian Gadd. Swift, *CE*, vol. 8, pp. 45–106.

——. *The Conduct of the Allies, and of the Late Ministry, in Beginning and Carrying on the Present War*. 1711. Edited by Herbert Davis. Swift, *PW* vol. 6, pp. 1–65.

——. *The Correspondence of Jonathan Swift*. Edited by Harold Williams, Clarendon P, 1963–65. 5 vols.

——. *The Correspondence of Jonathan Swift, D.D.* Edited by David Woolley, Peter

Lang, 1999–2014. 5 vols.

——. *A Discourse of the Contests and Dissensions between the Nobles and the Commons in Athens and Rome, with the Consequences They Had upon Both Those States*. 1701. Edited by Herbert Davis. Swift, *PW*, vol. 1, pp. 191–236.

——. *An Enquiry into the Behaviour of the Queen's Last Ministry, with Relation to Their Quarrells among Themselves, and the Design Charged upon Them of Altering the Succession of the Crown*. 1765. Edited by Herbert Davis and Irvin Ehrenpreis. Swift, *PW*, vol. 8, pp. 129–80.

——. *The Examiner*. 1710–11. Edited by Herbert Davis. Swift, *PW*, vol. 3, pp. 1–173.

——. 『「ガリヴァー旅行記」徹底注釈』（本文篇・注釈篇）富山太佳夫訳、原田範行・服部典之・武田将明注釈、岩波書店、2013 年。(Gulliver-ryoko-ki *tettei-chushaku* (Hombun-hen, chushaku-hen) [*Gulliver's Travels: A Thorough Annotation* (The Book of the Text and the Book of Annotations)]. Translated by Takao Tomiyama, annotated by Noriyuki Harada, Noriyuki Hattori, and Masaaki Takeda, Iwanami Shoten, 2013. In Japanese.)

——. *Gulliver's Travels*. 1726. Edited by Claude Rawson, notes by Ian Higgins, Oxford UP, 2005. Oxford World's Classics.

——. *Gulliver's Travels*. 1726. Edited by David Womersley. Swift, *CE*, vol. 15.

——. *Gulliver's Travels, 1726*. 1726. Edited by Herbert Davis, introduction by Harold Williams. Swift, *PW*, vol. 11.

——. *The History of the Four Last Years of the Queen*. 1758. Edited by Herbert Davis, introduction by Harold Williams. Swift, *PW*, vol. 7.

——. *Journal to Stella*. Edited by Harold Williams. 2 vols. Swift, *PW*, vols. 15–16.

——. *Journal to Stella: Letters to Esther Johnson and Rebecca Dingley, 1710–1713*. Edited by Abigail Williams. Swift, *CE*, vol. 9.

——. *A Letter from a Member of the House of Commons in Ireland to a Member of the House of Commons in England, concerning the Sacramental Test*. 1708. Edited by Herbert Davis. Swift, *PW*, vol. 2, pp. 109–25.

——. *Memoirs, Relating to That Change Which Happened in the Queen's Ministry in the Year 1710*. 1765. Edited by Herbert Davis and Irvin Ehrenpreis. Swift, *PW*, vol. 8, pp. 105–28.

——. *A Project for the Advancement of Religion, and the Reformation of Manners*. 1709. Edited by Herbert Davis. Swift, *PW*, vol. 2, pp. 41–63.

——. *The Prose Writings of Jonathan Swift*. General editor, Herbert Davis, Basil Blackwell, 1939–74. 16 vols.

——. *The Sentiments of a Church-of-England Man, with Respect to Religion and Government*. 1711. Edited by Herbert Davis. Swift, *PW*, vol. 2, pp. 1–25.

——. *Some Free Thoughts upon the Present State of Affairs*. 1741. Edited by Bertrand A. Goldgar and Ian Gadd. Swift, *CE*, vol. 8, pp. 289–311.

——. *Some Free Thoughts upon the Present State of Affairs*. 1741. Edited by Herbert Davis and Irvin Ehrenpreis. Swift, *PW*, vol. 8, pp. 73–98.

——. *A Tale of a Tub*. 1704. Edited by Marcus Walsh. Swift, *CE*, vol. 1, pp. 1–136.

——. *A Tale of a Tub*. 1704. Edited by Herbert Davis. Swift, *PW*, vol. 1, pp. xxxviii–xl, 1–135.

高濱俊幸『言語慣習と政治――ボーリングブルックの時代』木鐸社、1996 年。(Takahama, Toshiyuki. *Gengo-kanshu to seiji: Bolingbroke no jidai* [*Linguistic Convention and Politics: The Age of Bolingbroke*]. Bokutakusha, 1996. In Japanese.)

武田将明 (Takeda, Masaaki.) 解説『ロビンソン・クルーソー』、デフォー著、武田訳、河出書房新社、2011 年、463–99 頁 河出文庫テ 7-1。(Kaisetsu [Critical Commentary]. *Robinson Crusoe*, by Daniel Defoe, translated by Takeda, Kawade Shobo Shinsha, 2011, pp. 463–99. Kawade bunko Te-7-1. In Japanese.)

——.「名誉革命とフィクションの言説空間――デフォー作品における神意^{プロヴィデンス}の事後性」冨樫、313–63 頁。("Meiyo-kakumei to fiction no gensetsu-kukan: Defoe-sakuhin ni okeru Providence no jigo-sei" ["The Glorious Revolution and the Sphere of Discourse of Fiction: The Afterwardsness of Providence in Defoe's Works"]. Togashi, pp. 313–63. In Japanese.)

冨樫剛編『名誉革命とイギリス文学――新しい言説空間の誕生』春風社、2014 年。(Togashi, Go, editor. *Meiyo-kakumei to igirisu-bungaku: Atarashii gensetsu-kukan no tanjo* [*The Glorious Revolution and English Literature: The Rise of a New Sphere of Discourse*]. Shumpusha, 2014. In Japanese.)

Tuck, Richard. *Hobbes: A Very Short Introduction*. Oxford UP, 1989. Very Short Introductions.

Western, J. R. *Monarchy and Revolution: The English State in the 1680s*. Blandford P, 1972. Problems of History.

Weston, Corrine Comstock. *English Constitutional Theory and the House of Lords, 1556–1832*. 1965. Routledge, 2010. Routledge Revivals.

Williams, Harold. Introduction. Swift, *PW*, vol. 7, pp. ix–xxxvi.

山口孝道「ハリファックスの政治思想――名誉革命期の貴族政治思想の一例」『西洋史学』、119 号、1980 年、44–57 頁。(Yamaguchi, Takamichi. "Halifax no seiji-shiso: Meiyo-kakumei-ki no kizoku-seiji-shiso no ichirei" ["The Political Thought of the Marquess of Halifax: A Case of Aristocratic Ideas in the Period of the Glorious Revolution"]. *Seiyo shigaku* [*The Studies in Western History*], vol. 119, 1980, pp. 44–57. In Japanese.)

山崎時彦・山口孝道「ハリファックス──生涯と著作」『日和見主義者とは何か』、ハリファックス著、山崎・山口訳、未來社、1986 年、135–79 頁。(Yamasaki, Tokihiko, and Takamichi Yamaguchi. "Halifax: Shogai to chosaku" ["Halifax: His Life and Writings"]. *Hiyorimi-shugi-sha towa nani ka* [*The Character of a Trimmer*], by Marquess of Halifax [George Savile], translated by Yamasaki and Yamaguchi, Miraisha, 1986, pp. 135–79. In Japanese.)

Index

About the Author

Wataru Nakajima is Professor of English in the School of Commerce at Meiji University in Tokyo. He received his PhD from Sophia University, and his main research interests are eighteenth-century English literature and the history of political thought. His publications include coauthored books such as *Meiyo-kakumei to igirisu-bungaku: Atarashii gensetsu-kukan no tanjo* [*The Glorious Revolution and English Literature: The Rise of a New Sphere of Discourse*] (Shumpusha, 2014) and *Yoku wakaru igirisu-bungaku-shi* [*An Intelligible History of English Literature*] (Minerva Shobo, forthcoming in 2020), and many articles on Jonathan Swift and early modern English literature and thought. He has won the 19th Roggendorf Award from Soundings English Literary Association (2002); Honorable Mention for the 28th Young Scholar Award from the English Literary Society of Japan (2005); and the 17th Fukuhara Award (Research Grant Division) from the Fukuhara Memorial Fund for the Studies of English and American Literature (2009).

Academic Publication Series
of the Institute of Humaniries, Meiji University

明治大学人文科学研究所叢書

Jonathan Swift as a Conservative Trimmer:
An Ideological Reading of His English Politico-Religious Writings,
1701–1726

2020 年 2 月 2 日　初版発行

著　者　　中島　　渉

発行者　　福岡　正人

発行所　　株式会社 金星堂

（〒101–0051）東京都千代田区神田神保町 3–21
Tel. (03)3263–3828（営業部）
(03)3263–3997（編集部）
Fax (03)3263–0716
http://www.kinsei–do.co.jp

編集担当／佐藤求太
組版／ほんのしろ　装丁／興亜産業
印刷所／モリモト印刷　製本所／牧製本
落丁・乱丁本はお取り替えいたします
本書の内容を無断で複写・複製することを禁じます

©2020 Wataru Nakajima　Printed in Japan
ISBN978–4–7647–1196–9 C1098